THE SEVEN DARLINGS

"If there's any voting," said Phyllis, "I give my proxy to Gay"   [*See page* 161

THE
SEVEN DARLINGS

BY

GOUVERNEUR MORRIS

ILLUSTRATED BY

HOWARD CHANDLER CHRISTY

WILDSIDE PRESS

www.wildsidepress.com

TO

HOPE DAVIS

ILLUSTRATIONS

Illustrations

THE SEVEN DARLINGS

THE SEVEN DARLINGS

I

SIX of the Darlings were girls. The seventh was a young man who looked like Galahad and took exquisite photographs. Their father had died within the month, and Mr. Gilpin, the lawyer, had just faced them, in family assembled, with the lamentable fact that they, who had been so very, very rich, were now astonishingly poor.

"My dears," he said, "your poor father made a dreadful botch of his affairs. I cannot understand how some men——"

"Please!" said Mary, who was the oldest. "It can't be any satisfaction to know why we are poor. Tell us just how poor we are, and we'll make the best of it. I understand that The Camp isn't involved in the general wreck."

"It isn't," said Mr. Gilpin, "but you will have to sell it, or at least, rent it. Outside The Camp, when all the estate debts are paid, there will be thirty or forty thousand dollars to be divided among you."

The Seven Darlings

"In other words—*nothing*," said Mary; "I have known my father to spend more in a month."

"Income—" began Mr. Gilpin.

"*Dear* Mr. Gilpin," said Gay, who was the youngest by twenty minutes; "don't."

"Forty thousand dollars," said Mary, "at four per cent is sixteen hundred. Sixteen hundred divided by seven is how much?"

"Nothing," said Gay promptly. And all the family laughed, except Arthur, who was trying to balance a quill pen on his thumb.

"I might," said Mr. Gilpin helplessly, "be able to get you five per cent or even five and a half."

"You forget," said Maud, the second in age, and by some thought the first in beauty, "that we are father's children. Do you think *he* ever troubled his head about five and a half per cent, or even," she finished mischievously, "six?"

Arthur, having succeeded in balancing the quill for a few moments, laid it down and entered the discussion.

"What has been decided?" he asked. His voice was very gentle and uninterested.

"It's an awful pity mamma isn't in a position to help us," said Eve.

Eve was the third. After her, Arthur had been

The Seven Darlings

born; and then, all on a bright summer's morning, the triplets, Lee, Phyllis, and Gay.

"That old scalawag mamma married," said Lee, "spends all her money on his old hunting trips."

"Where is the princess at the moment?" asked Mr. Gilpin.

"They're in Somaliland," said Lee. "They almost took me. If they had, I shouldn't have called Oducalchi an old scalawag. You know the most dismal thing, when mamma and papa separated and *she* married *him*, was his turning out to be a regular old-fashioned brick. He can throw a fly yards further and lighter than any man *I* ever saw."

"And if you are bored," said Phyllis, "you say to him, 'Say something funny, Prince,' and he always can, instantly, without hesitation."

"All things considered," said Gay, "mamma's been a very lucky girl."

"Still," said Mary, "the fact remains that she's in no position to support us in the lap of luxury."

"Our kid brother," said Gay, "the future Prince Oducalchi, will need all she's got. When you realize that that child will have something like fifty acres of slate roofs to keep in order, it sets you thinking."

The Seven Darlings

"One thing I insist on," said Maud, "mamma shan't be bothered by a lot of hard-luck stories——"

"Did it ever occur to you, Mr. Gilpin," said Arthur, in his gentle voice, "that my sisters are the six sandiest and most beautiful girls in the world? I've been watching them out of the corner of my eye, and wishing to heaven that I were Romney or Gainsborough. I'd give a million dollars, if I had them, for their six profiles, immortally painted in a row. But nowadays if a boy has the impulse to be a painter, he is given a camera; or if he wishes to be a musician, he is presented with a pianola. Luxury is the executioner of art. Personally I am so glad that I am going to be poor that I don't know what to do."

"Aren't you sorry for us, Artie?" asked Gay.

"Very," said he; "and I don't like to be called Artie."

Immediately after their father's funeral the Darlings had hurried off to their camp on New Moon Lake. An Adirondack "camp" has much in common with a Newport "cottage." The Darlings' was no exception. There was nothing camp-like about it except its situation and the

The Seven Darlings

rough bark slats with which the sides of its buildings were covered. There were very many buildings. There was Darling House, in which the family had their sleeping-rooms and bathrooms and dressing-rooms. There was Guide's House, where the guides, engineers, and handy men slept and cooked, and loafed in rainy weather. A passageway, roofed but open at the sides, led from Darling House to Dining House—one vast room, in the midst of which an oval table which could be extended to seat twenty was almost lost. Heads of moose, caribou, and elk (not "caught" in the Adirondacks) looked down from the walls. Another room equally large adjoined this. It contained tables covered with periodicals; two grand pianos (so that Mary and Arthur could play duets without "bumping"); many deep and easy chairs, and a fireplace so large that when it was half filled with roaring logs it looked like the gates of hell, and was so called.

Pantry House and Bar House led from Dining House to Smoke House, where an olive-faced chef, all in white, was surrounded by burnished copper and a wonderful collection of blue and white.

There was Work House with its bench, forge,

and lathe for working wood and iron; Power House adjoining; and on the slopes of the mountain back of the camp, Spring House, from which water, ice-cold, at high pressure descended to circulate in the elaborate plumbing of the camp.

For guests, there were little houses apart—Rest House, two sleeping-rooms, a bath and a sitting-room; Lone House, in which one person could sleep, keep clean, write letters, or bask on a tiny balcony thrust out between the stems of two pine-trees and overhanging deep water; Bachelor House, to accommodate six of that questionable species. And placed here and there among pines that had escaped the attacks of nature and the greed of man were half a dozen other diminutive houses, accommodating from two to four persons.

The Camp was laid out like a little village. It had its streets, paved with pine-needles, its street lamps.

It had grown from simple beginnings with the Darling fortune; with the passing of this, it remained, in all its vast and intricate elaboration, like a white elephant upon the family's hands. From time to time they had tried the effect of giving the place a name, but had always come back to "The Camp." As such it was known the

The Seven Darlings

length and breadth of the North Woods. It was *The* Camp, par excellence, in a region devoted to camps and camping.

"Other people," the late Mr. Darling once remarked, "have more land, but nobody else has quite as much camp."

The property itself consisted of a long, narrow peninsula thrust far out into New Moon Lake, with half a mountain rising from its base. With the exception of a small village at the outlet of the lake, all the remaining lands belonged to the State, and since the State had no immediate use for them and since the average two weeks' campers could not get at them without much portage and expense, they were regarded by the Darlings as their own private preserves.

"The Camp," said Mr. Gilpin, "is, of course, a big asset. It is unique, and it is celebrated, at least among the people who might have the means to purchase it and open it. You could ask, and in time, I think, get a very large price."

They were gathered in the playroom. Mary, very tall and beautiful, was standing with her back to the fireplace.

"Mr. Gilpin," she said, "I have been coming to The Camp off and on for twenty-eight years. I will never consent to its being sold."

The Seven Darlings

"Nor I," said Maud. "Though I've only been coming for twenty-six."

"In twenty-four years," said Eve, "I have formed an attachment to the place which nothing can break."

"Arthur," appealed Mr. Gilpin, "perhaps you have some sense."

"I?" said Arthur. "Why? Twenty-two years ago I was born here."

"Good old Arthur!" exclaimed the triplets. "We were born here, too—just nineteen years ago."

"But," objected Mr. Gilpin, "you can't run the place—you can't live here. Confound it, you young geese, you can't even pay the taxes."

Lee whispered to Gay.

"Look at Mary!"

"Why?"

"She's got a look of father in her eyes—father going down to Wall Street to raise Cain."

Mary spoke very slowly.

"Mr. Gilpin," she said, "you are an excellent estate lawyer, and I am very fond of you. But you know nothing about finance. We are going to live here whenever we please. We are going to run it wide open, as father did. We are even going to pay the taxes."

The Seven Darlings

Mr. Gilpin was exasperated.

"Then you'll have to take boarders," he flung at her.

"Exactly," said Mary.

There was a short silence.

"How do you know," said Gay, "that they won't pick their teeth in public? I couldn't stand that."

"They won't be that kind," said Mary grimly. "And they will be so busy paying their bills that they won't have time."

"Seriously," said Arthur, "are you going to turn The Camp into an inn?"

"No," said Mary, "not into an inn. It has always been *The* Camp. We shall turn it into *The* Inn."

II

MR. GILPIN had departed in what had perhaps been the late Mr. Darling's last extravagant purchase, a motor-boat which at rest was a streak of polished mahogany, and at full speed, a streak of foam. The reluctant lawyer carried with him instructions to collect as much cash as possible and place it to the credit of the equally reluctant Arthur Darling.

"Arthur," Mary had agreed, "is perhaps the only one of us who could be made to understand that a bank account in his name is not necessarily at his own personal disposal. Arthur is altruistically and Don Quixotically honest."

It was necessary to warm the playroom with a tremendous fire, as October had changed suddenly from autumn to winter. There was a gusty grayness in the heavens that promised flurries of snow.

Since Mary's proposal of the day before to turn the expensive camp into a profitable inn, the family had talked of little else, and a number of ways and means had already been chosen from the innumerable ones proposed. In almost every instance Arthur had found himself an amused minority. His platform had been: "Make them comfortable at a fair price."

But Mary, who knew the world, had retorted:

"We are not appealing to people who consider what they pay but to people who only consider what they get. Make them luxurious; and they will pay anything we choose to ask."

After Mr. Gilpin's chillsome departure in the *Streak*, the family resumed the discussion in front of the great fire in the playroom. Wow, the dog, who had been running a deer for twenty-four hours in defiance of all game-laws, was present in the flesh, but his weary spirit was in the land of dreams, as an occasional barking and bristling of his mane testified. Uncas, the chipmunk, had also demanded and received admittance to the council. For a time he had sat on Arthur's shoulder, puffing his cheeks with inconceivable rapidity, then, soporifically inclined by the warmth of the fire and the constant strain incident to his attempts to understand the ins and outs of the English language when rapidly and even slangily spoken, he dropped into Arthur's breast-pocket and went to sleep.

Arthur sighed. He was feeling immensely

fidgety; but he knew that any sudden, irritable shifting of position would disturb the slumbers of Uncas, and so for nearly an hour he held himself heroically, almost uncannily, still.

Two years ago, dating from his graduation, Arthur had had a change of heart. He had been so dissipated as to give his family cause for the utmost anxiety. He had squandered money with both hands. He had had a regular time for lighting a cigarette, namely, when the one which he had been smoking was ready to be thrown away. He had been a keen hunter and fisherman. His chief use for domestic animals was to tease them and play tricks upon them. Then suddenly, out of this murky sky, had shone the clear light of all his subsequent behavior. He neither drank nor smoked; he neither slaughtered deer nor caught fish. He was never quarrelsome. He went much into the woods to photograph and observe. He became almost too quiet and self-effacing for a young man. He asked nothing of the world—not even to be let alone. He was patient under the fiendish ministrations of bores. He tamed birds and animals, spoiling them, as grandparents spoil grandchildren, until they gave him no peace, and were always running to him at inconvenient times because they were hungry, because they were sleepy, because they thought somebody had been abusing them, or because they wished to be tickled and amused.

"He's like a peaceful lake," Maud had once said, "deep in the woods, where the wind never blows," and Eve had nodded and said: "True. And there's a woman at the bottom of it."

The sisters all believed that Arthur's change of heart could be traced to a woman. They differed only as to the kind.

"One of our kind," Mary thought, "who wouldn't have him."

"One of our kind," thought Maud, "who couldn't have him."

And the triplets thought differently every day. All except Gay, who happened to know.

"But," said Maud, "if we are to appeal to people of our own class, all mamma's and papa's old friends and our own will come to us, and that will be much, too much, like charity."

"Right," said Mary. "Don't tell *me* I haven't thought of that. I have. Applications from old friends will be politely refused."

"We can say," said Eve, "that we are very sorry, but every room is taken."

"But suppose they aren't?" objected Arthur.

Eve retorted sharply.

The Seven Darlings

"What is that to do with it? We are running a business, not a Bible class."

But Phyllis was pulling a long face.

"Aren't we ever to see any of our old friends any more?"

Lee and Gay nudged each other and began to tease her.

"Dearest Pill," they said, "all will yet be well. There is more than one Geoffrey Plantagenet in the world. You shall have the pick of all the handsome strangers."

"Oh, come, now!" said Arthur, "Phyllis is right. Now and then we must have guests—who don't pay."

"Not until we can afford them," said Mary. "Has anybody seen the sketch-map that papa made of the buildings?"

"I know where it is," said Arthur, "but I can't get it now; because Wow needs my feet for a pillow and at the moment Uncas is very sound asleep."

"Can't you *tell* us where it is?"

"Certainly," he said; "it's in the safe. The safe is locked."

"And where is the key?"

"Just under Uncas."

"Very well, then," said Mary, "important

business must wait until Stripes wakes up. Meanwhile, I think we ought to make up our minds how and how much to advertise."

"There are papers," said Eve, "that all wealthy Americans always see, and then there's that English paper with all the wonderful advertisements of country places for sale or to let. I vote for a full-page ad in that. People will say, 'Jove, this must be a wonderful proposition if it pays 'em to advertise it in an English paper.'"

Everybody agreed with Eve except Arthur. He merely smiled with and at her.

"We can say," said Eve, "shooting and fishing over a hundred thousand acres. Does the State own as much as that, Arthur?"

He nodded, knowing the futility of arguing with the feminine conscience.

"Two hundred thousand?"

He nodded again.

"Then," said Eve, "make a note of this, somebody." Maud went to the writing-table. "Shooting and fishing over hundreds of thousands of acres."

"There must be pictures," said Maud, "in the text of the ad—the place is full of them; and if they won't do, Arthur can take others—when Wow and Uncas wake up."

The Seven Darlings

"There must be that picture after the opening of the season," said Mary, "the year the party got nine bucks—somebody make a point of finding that picture."

"There are some good strings of trout and bass photographically preserved," said Gay.

"A picture of chef in his kitchen will appeal," said Lee.

"So will interiors," said Maud. "Bedrooms with vistas of plumbing. Let's be honestly grateful to papa for all the money he spent on porcelain and silver plate."

"Oh, come," said Mary, "we must advertise in the American papers, too. I think we should spend a good many thousand dollars. And of course we must do away with the big table in the dining-house and substitute little tables. I propose that we ransack the place for photographs, and that Maud try her hand at composing full-page ads. And, Arthur, please don't forget the sketch plan of the buildings—we'll have to make quite a lot of alterations."

"I've thought of something," said Maud. "Just a line. Part of the ad, of course, mentions prices. Now I think if we say prices from so and so up—it looks cheap and commonplace. At the bottom of the ad, then, after we've described all

The Seven Darlings

the domestic comforts of The Camp and its sporting opportunities, let's see if we can't catch the *clientèle* we are after with this:

"'Prices Rather High.'"

"Maud," said Mary, after swift thought, "your mind is as clear as a gem. Just think how that line would have appealed to papa if he'd been looking into summer or winter resorts. Make a note of it— What are you two whispering about?"

Lee and Gay looked up guiltily. They had not only been whispering but giggling. They said: "Nothing. Absolutely nothing."

But presently they put on sweaters and rowed off in a guide boat, so that they might converse without fear of being observed.

"Sure you've got it?" asked Lee.

"Umm," said Gay, "sure."

They giggled.

"And you think we're not just plain conceited?"

"My dear Lee," said Gay, "Mary, Maud, and Eve are famous for their faces and their figgers— have been for years, poor old things. Well, in my candid opinion, you and Phyllis are better-looking in every way. I look at you two from the

17

cool standpoint of a stranger, and I tell you that you are incomparably good-looking."

Lee laughed with mischievous delight.

"And you look so exactly like us," she said, "that strangers can't tell us apart."

"For myself," said Gay demurely, "I claim nothing. Absolutely nothing. But you and Pill are certainly as beautiful as you are young."

"For the sake of argument, then," said Lee, "let's admit that we six sisters considered as a collection are somewhat alluring to the eye. Well—when the mail goes with the ads Maud is making up, we'll go with it, and make such changes in the choice of photographs as we see fit."

"That won't do," said Gay. "There will be proofs to correct."

"Then we'll wait till the proofs are corrected and sent off."

"Yes. That will be the way. It would be a pity for the whole scheme to fall through for lack of brains. I suppose the others would never agree?"

"The girls *might*," said Lee, "but Arthur never. He would rise up like a lion. You know, deep down in his heart he's a frightful stickler for the proprieties."

"We shall get ourselves into trouble."

The Seven Darlings

"It will not be the first or the last time. And besides, we can escape to the woods if necessary, like Bessie Belle and Mary Grey."

"Who were they?"

> " 'They were two bonnie lassies.
> They built a house on yon burn brae
> And thecht it o'er wi' rashes.' "

III

IF we except Arthur, whose knowledge of the Adirondack woods and waters was that of a naturalist, Lee and Gay were the sportsmen of the family. They had begun to learn the arts of fishing and hunting from excellent masters at the tender age of five. They knew the deeps and shallows of every lake and brook within many miles as intimately as a good housewife knows the shelves in her linen closet. They talked in terms of blazes, snags, spring holes, and runways. Each owned a guide boat, incomparably light, which she could swing to her shoulders and carry for a quarter of a mile without blowing. If Lee was the better shot, Gay could throw the more seductive fly.

There had been a guide in the girls' extreme youth, a Frenchman, Pierre Amadis de Troissac, who had perhaps begun life as a gentleman. Whatever his history, he had taught the precious pair the rudiments of French and the higher mysteries of fishing.

The Seven Darlings

He had made a special study of spring holes, an essential in Adirondack trout-fishing, and whenever the Darlings wanted trout, it had only been necessary to tell De Troissac how many they wanted and to wait a few hours. On those occasions when he went fishing for the larder, Lee and Gay, two little roly-polies with round, innocent eyes, often accompanied him. It never occurred to De Troissac that the children could mark down the exact places from which he took fish, and, one by one and quite unintentionally, he revealed to them the hard-won secrets of his spring holes. The knowledge, however, went no further. They would have told Phyllis, of course, if she had been a sport. But she wasn't. She resembled Lee and Gay almost exactly in all other ways; but the spirit of pursuit and capture was left out of her. Twice she had upset a boat because a newly landed bass had suddenly begun to flop in the bottom of it, and once, coming accidentally upon a guide in the act of disembowelling a deer, she had gone into hysterics. She could row, carry a boat, swim, and find the more travelled trails; but, as Lee and Gay said: "Pill would starve in the woods directly the season was over."

She couldn't discharge even a twenty-two

calibre rifle without shutting her eyes; she couldn't throw a fly twenty feet without snarling her leader. The more peaceful arts of out-of-doors had excited her imagination and latent skill.

In the heart of the woods, back of The Camp, not to be seen or even suspected until you came suddenly upon it, she had an acre of gardens under exquisite cultivation, and not a little glass. She specialized in nectarines, white muscats of Alexandria, new peas, and heaven-blue larkspur. But, for the sake of others, she grew to perfection beets, sweet corn, the lilies in variety, and immense Japanese iris.

As The Camp was to be turned into an inn which should serve its guests with delicious food, Phyllis and her garden became of immense importance and she began to sit much apart, marking seed catalogues with one end of a pencil and drumming on her beautiful teeth with the other.

Negotiations had been undertaken with a number of periodicals devoted to outdoor life, and a hundred schemes for advertising had been boiled down to one, which even Arthur was willing to let stand. To embody Mary's ideas of a profitable proposition into a page of advertising without being too absurd or too "cheap," had proved extremely difficult.

"We will run The Inn," she said, "so that rich people will live very much as they would if they were doing the running. One big price must cover all the luxuries of home. We must eliminate all extras—everything which is a nuisance or a trouble. Except for the trifling fact that we receive pay for it, we must treat them exactly as papa used to treat his guests. He gave his guests splendid food of his own ordering. When they wanted cigars or cigarettes, they helped themselves. There was always champagne for dinner, but if men preferred whiskey and soda, they told the butler, and he saw that they got it. What I'm driving at is this: There must be no difference in price for a guest who drinks champagne and one who doesn't drink anything. And more important still, we must do all the laundering without extra charge; guides, guide boats, guns, and fishing-tackle must be on tap— just as papa had everything for his guests. The one big price must include absolutely everything."

Added to this general idea, it was further conveyed in the final advertisement that the shooting was over hundreds of thousands of acres and the fishing in countless lakes and streams. And the last line of the ad, as had been previously agreed, was this:

"PRICES RATHER HIGH."

And, as Gay said to Lee: "If that doesn't fetch 'em—you and I know something that maybe will."

The full-page ad began and ended with a portrait of Uncas, the chipmunk, front view, sitting up, his cheeks puffed to the bursting point. The centre of the page was occupied by a rather large view of The Camp and many of the charming little buildings which composed it, taken from the lake. Throughout the text were scattered reproductions—strings of trout, a black bear, nine deer hanging in a row, and other seductions to an out-of-door life. For lovers of good food there was a tiny portrait of the chef and adjoining it a photograph of the largest bunch of white muscats that had ever matured in Phyllis's vinery.

A few days before the final proofs began to come in from the advertising managers, there arrived, addressed to Gay, a package from a firm in New York which makes a specialty of developing and printing photographs for amateurs. Gay concealed the package, but Lee had noted its existence, and sighed with relief. A little later she found occasion to take Gay aside.

"Was the old film all right? Did they print well?"

Gay nodded. "It always was a wonderful picture," she said.

"Us for the tall timber," she said—"when they come out."

The final proofs being corrected and enveloped, Gay and Lee, innocent and bored of face, announced that, as there was nothing to do, they thought they would row the mail down to the village. It was a seven-mile row, but that was nothing out of the ordinary for them and it was arranged that the *Streak* should be sent after them in case they showed signs of being late for lunch.

Gay rowed with leisurely strokes, while Lee, seated in the stern, busied herself with a pair of scissors and a pot of paste. She was giving the finally corrected proofs that still more final correcting which she and Gay had agreed to be necessary.

They had decided that the centrepiece of the advertisement—a mere general view of The Camp—though very charming in its way, "meant nothing," and they had made up their unhallowed minds to substitute in its place one of those "fortunate snap-shots," the film of which Gay had —happened to preserve.

In this photograph the six Darling sisters were seated in a row, on the edge of The Camp float. Their feet and ankles were immersed. They wore black bathing-dresses, exactly alike, and the bathing-dresses were of rather thin material —and very, very wet.

The six exquisite heads perched on the six exquisite figures proved a picture which, as Lee and Gay admitted, might cause even a worthy young man to leave home and mother.

It was not until they were half-way home that Lee suddenly cried aloud and hid her face in her hands.

"For Heaven's sake," exclaimed Gay, "trim boat, and what's the matter anyway?"

"Matter?" exclaimed Lee; "that picture of us sits right on top of the line *Prices Rather High*. And it's too late to do anything about it!"

Gay turned white and then red, and then she burst out laughing. " 'Tis awful," she said, "but it will certainly fetch 'em."

IV

THE CAMP itself underwent numerous changes during the winter; and even the strong-hearted Mary was appalled by the amount of money which it had been found necessary to expend. The playroom would, of course, be reserved for the use of guests, and a similar though smaller and inferior room had been thrust out from the west face of Darling House for the use of the family. Then Maud, who had volunteered to take charge of all correspondence and accounts, had insisted that an office be built for her near the dock. This was mostly shelves, a big fireplace, and a table. Here guests would register upon arrival; here the incoming mail would be sorted and the outgoing weighed and stamped. It had also been found necessary, in view of the very large prospective wash, to enlarge and renovate Laundry House and provide sleeping quarters for a couple of extra laundresses.

Those who are familiar with the scarcity and reluctance of labor in the Adirondacks will best understand how these trifling matters bit into the Darling capital.

The Seven Darlings

Sometimes Mary, who held herself responsible for the possible failure of the projected inn, could not sleep at night. Suppose that the advertising, which would cost thousands of dollars, should fall flat? Suppose that not a single solitary person should even nibble at the high prices? The Darlings might even find themselves dreadfully in debt. The Camp would have to go. She suffered from nightmares, which are bad, and from daymares, which are worse. Then one day, brought across the ice from the village of Carrytown at the lower end of the lake, she received the following letter:

Miss Darling,
    The Camp, New Moon Lake in the Adirondacks, New York.
    Dear Madam:—Yesterday morning, quite by accident, I saw the prospectus of your inn on the desk of Mr. Burns, the advertising manager of *The Four Seasons*. I note with regret that you are not opening until the first of July. Would it not be possible for you to receive myself and a party of guests very much earlier, say just when the ice has gone out of the lake and the trout are in the warm shallows along the shores? Personally, it is my plan to stay on with you for the balance of the season, provided, of course, that all your accommodations have not been previously taken.
    With regard to prices, I note only that they are "rather high." I would suggest that, as it would

28

The Seven Darlings

probably inconvenience you to receive guests prior to the date set for the formal opening of your camp, you name a rate for three early weeks which would be profitable to you. There will be six men in my party, including myself.

Very truly yours,

Samuel Langham.

Mary, her face flushed with the bright colors of triumph, read this letter aloud to the assembled family.

"Does anybody," she asked, "know anything about Samuel Langham? Is he a suitable person?"

"I know of him," said Arthur, smiling at some recollection or other. "He is what the newspapers call a 'well-known clubman.' He is rich, fat, good-natured, and not old. It is that part of your prospectus which touches upon the *cuisine* that has probably affected him. His father was a large holder of Standard Oil securities."

"As for me," said Gay, "I've seen him. Do you remember, Phyllis, being asked to a most 'normous dinner dance at the Redburns' the year we came out? At the last minute you caught cold and wanted to back out, but Mary said *that* wasn't done, and so I went in your place, and, as usual, nobody knew the difference. Well, Mr. Langham was there. I didn't meet him, but I remember I watched him eat. He is very smug-looking. He didn't like the champagne. I remember that. He lifted his glass hopefully, took one swallow, put his glass down, and never touched it again. His face for the rest of dinner had the expression of one who has been deeply wronged. I thought of Louis XVI mounting the scaffold."

"I do wish," said Mary, "that we knew what kind of wine the creature likes."

"Father left a splendid collection," said Arthur. "Take Mr. Langham into the cellar. He'll enjoy that. Let him pick his own bottle."

In the event, Maud sat down in her new office and wrote Mr. Langham that he and his five guests could be received earlier in the season. And then, with fear and trembling, she named a price *per diem* that amounted to highway robbery.

Mr. Langham's answer was prompt and cheerful. He asked merely to be notified when the ice had gone out of the lake.

"Well," said Mary, with a long-drawn sigh of relief, "the prices don't seem to have frightened him nearly as much as they frightened us. But, after all, the prospectus was alluring—though we say it that shouldn't."

Lee and Gay were troubled by qualms of conscience. The advertisements of The Camp were

The Seven Darlings

to appear in the February number of some of the more important periodicals, and the two scapegraces were beginning to be horribly alarmed.

Magazines have a way of being received last by those most interested in seeing them. And before even a copy of *The Four Seasons* reached the Darlings, there came a number of letters from people who had already seen the advertisement in it. One letter was from a very old friend of the family, and ran as follows:

My Dear Mary:

How could you! I have seen your advertisement of The Camp in *The Four Seasons*. It is earning much talk and criticism. I don't know what you could have been thinking of. I have always regarded you as one of the sanest and best-bred women I know. But it seems that you are not above sacrificing your own dignity to financial gain——

"Well, in the name of all that's ridiculous," exclaimed Mary; "of all that's impertinent!—will somebody kindly tell me what my personality has to do with our prospectus of The Camp?"

Those who could have told her held their tongues and quaked inwardly. The others joined in Mary's surprise and indignation. Even Arthur, who hated the whole innkeeping scheme, was roused out of his ordinary placidity.

The Seven Darlings

"I shall write to the horrid old woman," said Mary, "and tell her to mind her own business. I shall also tell her that we are receiving so many applications for accommodations that we don't know how to choose. That isn't quite true, of course; but we have received some. Since I am not above sacrificing my dignity"—she went on angrily—"to financial gain, I may as well throw a few lies into the bargain."

The next day, addressed to "The Camp," came the long-expected number of *The Four Seasons*. Arthur opened it and began to turn the leaves. Presently, from the centre of a page, he saw his six beautiful sisters looking him in the face.

"Mary!" he called, in such a voice that she came running. She looked and turned white. Eve came, and Maud and Phyllis.

"Who is responsible for this—" cried Arthur, "for this sickening—this degraded piece of mischief?"

"You corrected the final proofs yourself," said Maud.

"And sealed them up. If I find that some mischief-maker in the office of *The Four Seasons* has been playing tricks——"

"The mischief-makers are to be found nearer home," said Mary. "Don't you remember that

The Seven Darlings

Lee and Gay took the proofs to the post-office. They said they were bored and could think of nothing to do. *This* is what they were thinking of doing!"

"Where are they?" he said in a grim voice.

"Now, Arthur," said Maud, "think before you say anything to them that you may regret. As for the picture of us in our bathing-suits— well, I, for one, don't see anything dreadful about it. In fact, I think we look rather lovely."

Arthur groaned.

"I want to talk to Lee and Gay," he said. "My sisters—an advertisement in a magazine —for drummers and newsboys to make jokes about——"

He grew white and whiter, until his innocent sisters were thoroughly frightened. Then he started out of the playroom in search of Lee and Gay.

In or about The Camp they were not to be found. Nobody had seen them since breakfast. With this information, he returned to the play-room.

"They've run away," he said, "and I'm going after them."

"I wouldn't," said Mary. "The harm's been done. You can't very well spank them. I wish you could. You can only scold—and what earthly good will that do them, or you?"

"I don't know that anything I may say," said Arthur, "*will* do them any good. I live in hopes."

"Have you any idea where they've gone?"

"I'll cast about in a big circle and find their tracks."

When Arthur, mittened and snow-shoed, had departed in search of Lee and Gay, the remaining sisters gathered about the full-page advertisement in *The Four Seasons,* and passed rapidly from anger to mild hysterics. Mary was the last to laugh.

And she said: "Girls, I will tell you an awful secret. I never would have consented to this, but as long as Lee and Gay have gone and done it, I'm—*glad.*"

"The only thing *I* mind," said Eve, "is Arthur. He'll take it hard."

"We can't help that," said Maud. "Business is business. And this wretched, shocking piece of mischief spells success. I feel it in my bones. There's no use being silly about ourselves. We've got our way to make in the world—and, as a sextet——"

She lingered over the picture.

The Seven Darlings

"As a sextet, there's no use denying that we are rather lovely to look at."

Phyllis put in a word blindly.

"Maud," she said, "among the applications you have received, how many are from women?"

Maud laughed aloud.

"None," she said.

"There wouldn't be," said Eve.

"Well," said Mary, "compared to the rest of you, I'm quite an old woman, and I say—so much the better."

V

EVEN on going into the open air from a warmed room, it would not have struck you as a cold day. But thermometers marked a number of degrees worse than zero. The sky was bright and blue. Not a breath of wind stirred. In the woods the underbrush was hidden by the smooth accumulations of snow, so that the going was open.

The Adirondack winter climate is such that a man runs less risk of getting too cold than of getting too warm. Arthur, moving swiftly in a great circle so that at some point he should come upon the tracks of his culprit sisters, shed first his mittens and then his coat. The former he thrust into his trousers pocket, and he hung the latter to a broken limb where he could easily find it on his return.

"There would be some sense in running away in summer," he thought. "It would take an Indian or a dog to track them then, but in winter —I gave them credit for more sense."

He came upon the outgoing marks of their

The Seven Darlings

snow-shoes presently, just beyond Phyllis's garden, to the north of the camp. In imagination he saw the two lithe young beauties striding sturdily and tirelessly over the snow, and then and there the extreme pinnacles of his anger toppled and fell. There is no occupation to which a maiden may lend herself so virginal as woodmanship. And he fell to thinking less of his young sisters' indiscretion than of the extreme and unsophisticated innocence which had led them into it. What could girls know of men, anyway? What did his sisters know of him? That he had been extravagant and rather fast. Had they an inkling of what being rather fast meant? His smooth forehead contracted with painful thoughts. Even Mary's indignation upon the discovery of the photograph in *The Four Seasons* had not matched his own. She had been angry because she was a gentlewoman, and gentlewomen shun publicity. She had not even guessed at the degradation to which broadcast pictures of beautiful women are subjected. His anger turned from his sisters presently and glowered upon the whole world of men; his hands closed to strike, and opened to clutch and choke. That Lee and Gay had done such a thing was earnest only of innocence coupled with mischief. They must know that what they had done was wrong, since they had fled from any immediate consequences, but how wrong it was they could never dream, even in nightmares. Nor was it possible for him to explain. How, then, could any anger which he might visit upon them benefit? And who was he, when it came to that, to assume the unassailable morality of a parent?

It came to this: That Arthur followed the marks of Lee's and Gay's snow-shoes mechanically, and raged, not against them, not against the world of men, but against himself. He had said once in jest that many an artistic impulse had been crushed by the camera and the pianola. But how pitifully true this had been in his own case! If he had been born into less indulgence, he might have painted, he might have played. The only son in a large family of daughters, his father and mother had worshipped the ground upon which his infant feet had trod. He had never known what it was to want anything. He had never been allowed to turn a hand to his own honest advantage. He was the kind of boy who, under less golden circumstances, would have saved his pocket-money and built with his own hands a boat or whatever he needed. There is a song: "I want what I want when I want it."

The Seven Darlings

Arthur might have sung: "I get what I'm going to want and then I don't want it."

His contemporaries had greatly envied him, when, as a mere matter of justice, they should have pitied him. All his better impulses had been gnarled by indulgence. He had done things that showed natural ability; but of what use was that? He was too old now to learn to draw. He played rather delightfully upon the piano, or any other instrument, for that matter. To what end? He could not read a note.

There was nothing that Arthur could not have done, if he had been let alone. There were many things that he would have done.

At college he had seen in one smouldering flash of intuition how badly he had started in the race of life. When others were admiring his many brilliancies, he was mourning for the lost years when, under almost any guidance save that of his beloved father, he might have laid such sturdy foundations to future achievements—pedestals on which to erect statues.

Self-knowledge had made him hard for a season and cynical. As a tired sea-gull miscalculates distance and dips his wings into the sea, so Arthur, when he thought that he was merely flying low the better to see and to observe, had alighted

The Seven Darlings

without much struggling in a pool of dissipation
and vice.

The memory was more of a weariness to him
than a sharp regret. Of what use is remorse—
after the fact ? Let it come before and all will be
well.

At last, more by accident than design, he drew
out of the muddy ways into which he had fallen
and limped off—not so much toward better things
as away from worse.

Then it was that Romance had come for him,
and carried him on strong wings upward toward
the empyrean.

Even now, she was only twenty. She had
married a man more than twice her age. He
had been her guardian, and she had felt that it
was her duty. Her marriage proved desperately
unhappy. She and Arthur met, and, as upon a
signal, loved.

For a few weeks of one golden summer, they
had known the ethereal bliss of seeing each other
every day. They met as little children, and so
parted. They accepted the law and convention
which stood between them, not as a barrier to be
crossed or circumvented but with childlike faith
as a something absolutely impassable—like the
space which separates the earth and the moon.

The Seven Darlings

They remained utterly innocent in thought and deed, merely loved and longed and renounced so very hard that their poor young hearts almost broke.

Not so the "old man."

It happened, in the autumn of that year, that he brought his wife to New York, in whose Wall Street he had intricate interests. He learned that she was by way of seeing more of Arthur than a girl of eighteen married to a man of nearly fifty ought to see. He did not at once burst into coarse abuse of her, but, worldly-wise, set detectives to watch her. He had, you may say, set his heart upon her guilt. To learn that she was utterly innocent enraged him. One day he had the following conversation with a Mr. May, of a private detective bureau:

"You followed them?"

"To the park."

"Well?"

"They bought a bag of peanuts and fed the squirrels."

"Go on."

"Then they rode in a swan-boat. Then they walked up to the reservoir and around it. Then they came back to the hotel."

"Did they separate in the office?"

The Seven Darlings

"On the sidewalk."

"But last night? She said she was dining with her sister and going to the play. What did she do last night?"

"She did what she said. Believe me, sir—if I know anything of men and women, you're paying me to run fool's errands for you. *They* don't need any watching."

"You have seen them—kiss?"

"Never."

"Hold hands?"

"I haven't seen any physical demonstration. I guess they like each other a lot. And that's all there is to it."

But the "old man" made a scene with her, just such a scene as he would have made if the detective's report had been, in effect, the opposite of what it was. He assumed that she was guilty; but, for dread of scandal, he would not seek a divorce. He exacted a promise that she would not see Arthur, or write to him, or receive letters from him.

Then, having agreed with certain magnates to go out to China upon the question of a great railroad and a great loan, he carried her off with him, then and there. So that when Arthur called at the hotel, he was told that they had gone but

The Seven Darlings

that there was a note for him.   If it was from the
wife, the husband had dictated it:

Don't try to see me ever any more.   If you do, it
will only make my life a hell on earth.

That had been the tangible end of Arthur's
romance.   But the intangible ends were infinite
and not yet.   His whole nature had changed.
He had suffered and could no longer bear to in-
flict pain.

He lifted his head and looked up a little slope
of snow.   Near the top, wonderfully rosy and
smiling, sat his culprit sisters.   He had forgotten
why he had come. . He smiled in his sudden embarrassment.

"Don't shoot, colonel," called Gay, "and we'll
come down."

"Promise, then," he said, "that you'll never be
naughty again."

"We promise," they said.

And they trudged back to camp, with jokes
and laughter and three very sharp appetites.

VI

BEYOND seeing to it that the alluring picture of his sisters should not appear in any future issues of the magazines, Arthur did not refer to the matter again. The girls, more particularly Lee and Gay, always attributed the instant success of The Camp to the picture; but it is sanely possible that an inn run upon such very extravagant principles was bound to be a success anyway. America is full of people who will pay anything for the comforts of home with the cares and exasperations left out.

A majority of the early applications received at The Camp office, and politely rejected by Maud, were from old friends of the family, who were eagerly willing to give its fallen finances a boost. But the girls were determined that their scheme should stand upon its own meritorious feet or not at all.

When Samuel Langham learned that the ice was going out of New Moon Lake, he wrote that he would arrive at Carrytown at such and such

The Seven Darlings

an hour, and begged that a boat of some sort might be there to meet him. His guests, he explained, would follow in a few days.

"Dear me," said Maud, "it will be very trying to have him alone—just like a real guest. If he'd only bring his friends with him, why, they could entertain him. As it is, we'll have to. Because, even if we are innkeepers now, we belong to the same station in life that he does, and he knows it and we know it. I don't see how we can ever have the face to send in a bill afterward."

"I don't either," said Mary, "but we must."

"I've never pictured him," said Arthur, "as a man who would brave early spring in the Adirondacks for the sake of a few trout."

"I bet you my first dividend," said Lee, "that his coat is lined with sable."

It was.

As the *Streak*, which had gone to Carrytown to meet him, slid for the dock (his luggage was to follow in the *Tortoise*, a fatter, slower power-boat), there might have been seen standing amidships a tall, stout gentleman of about thirty-six or more, enveloped in a handsome overcoat lined with sable.

He wore thick eye-glasses which the swiftness of the *Streak's* going had opaqued with icy mist, so that for the moment Mr. Samuel Langham was blind as a mole. Nevertheless, determined to enjoy whatever the experience had in store for him, he beamed from right to left, as if a pair of keen eyes were revealing to him unexpected beauties and delights.

Arthur, loathing the rôle, was on the float to meet him.

On hearing himself addressed by name, Mr. Samuel Langham removed one of his fur-lined gloves and thrust forward a plump, well-groomed hand.

"I believe that I am shaking hands with Mr. Darling," he said in a slow, cultivated voice; "but my glasses are blurred and I cannot see anything. Is my foot going for the float—or the water?"

"Step boldly," said Arthur; and, in a hurried aside, as he perceived the corner of a neatly folded greenback protruding between two of Mr. Langham's still-gloved fingers: "You are not to be subjected to the annoyance of the tipping system. We pay our servants extra to make the loss up to them."

Mr. Langham's mouth, which was rather like a Cupid's bow, tightened. And he handed the greenback to the engineer of the *Streak*, just as if Ar-

thur's remonstrance had not been spoken. On
the way to the office he explained.

"Whenever I go anywhere," he said, "I find
persons in humble situations who smile at me and
wish me well. I smile back and wish them well.
It is because, at some time or other, I have
tipped them. To me the system has never been an
annoyance but a delightful opportunity for the
exercise of tact and judgment."

He came to a dead halt, planting his feet firmly.

"I shall be allowed to tip whomsoever I like,"
he said flatly, "or I shan't stay."

"Our ambition," said Arthur stiffly, "is to make
our guests comfortable. Our rule against tipping
is therefore abolished."

They entered the office. Mr. Langham could
now see, having wiped the fog from his glasses.
He saw a lovely girl in black, seated at a table
facing him. Beyond her was a roaring fire of
backlogs. Arthur presented Mr. Langham.

"Are you frozen?" asked Maud. "Too cold
to write your name in our brand-new register?"

He took the pen which she offered him and wrote
his name in a large, clear hand, worthy of John
Hancock.

"It's the first name in the book," he said.

The Seven Darlings

"It's always been a very lucky name for me. I hope it will be for you."

Arthur had escaped.

"There is one more formality," said Maud: "breakfast."

"I had a little something in my car," said Mr. Langham; "but if it wouldn't be too much trouble —er—just a few little eggs and things."

"How would it be," said Maud, "if I took you straight to the kitchen? My sister Mary presides there, and you shall tell her exactly what you want, and she will see that you get it."

A rosy blush mounted Mr. Langham's good-natured face.

"Oh," he said, with the deepest sincerity, "if I am to have the *entrée* to the kitchen, I shall be happy. I will tell you a secret. At my club I always breakfast in the kitchen. It's against the rules, but I do it. A friendly chef—beds of glowing charcoal—burnished copper—piping-hot tidbits."

It was uphill to Smoke House, and Mr. Langham, in his burdensome overcoat, grew warm on the way, and was puffing slightly when he got there.

"Mary," Maud called—"Mr. Langham!"

"The kitchen is the foundation of all domestic

48

The Seven Darlings

happiness," said he. "I have come to yours as fast as I could. I think—I *know*, that I never saw a brighter, happier-looking kitchen."

He knew also that he had never seen so beautiful a presiding deity.

"Your sister," he said, "told me that I could have a little breakfast right here." And he repeated the statement concerning his club kitchen.

"Of course, you can!" said Mary.

"Just a few eggs," he said, "and if there's anything green——"

They called the chef. He was very happy because the season had begun. He assigned Mr. Langham a seat from which to see and at which to be served, then with the wrist-and-finger elegance of a prestidigitator, he began to prepare a few eggs and something green.

"The trout——" Mary began dutifully, as it was for the sake of these that Mr. Langham had ostensibly come so early in the season.

"Trout?" he said.

"The fishing——" She made a new beginning.

"The fishing, Miss Darling," he said, "will be of interest to my friends. For my part, I don't fish. I have, in common with the kind of boat from which fishing is done, nothing but the fact that we are both ticklish. I saw your prospectus.

49

The Seven Darlings

I said: 'I shall be happy there, and well taken care of.' Something told me that I should be allowed to breakfast in the kitchen. The more I thought about it the less I felt that I could wait for the somewhat late opening of your season, so I pretended to be a fisher of trout. And here I am. But, mark you," he added, "a few trout on the table now and then—I like that!"

"You shall have them," said Mary, "and you shall breakfast in the kitchen. I do—always."

"Do you?" he exclaimed. "Why not together, then?"

His eyes shone with pleasure.

"I should be too early for you," she said.

"You don't know me. Is it ever too early to eat? Because I am stout, people think I have all the moribund qualities that go with it. As a matter of fact, I rise whenever, in my judgment, the cook is dressed and down. Is it gross to be fond of food? So many people think so. I differ with them. Not to care what you eat is gross—in my way of thinking. Is there anything, for instance, more fresh in coloring, more adequate in line, than a delicately poached egg on a blue-and-white plate? You call this building Smoke House? I shall always be looking in. Do you mind?"

The Seven Darlings

"Indeed we don't," said Mary. "Do we, chef?"

Chef laid a finger to his lips. It was no time for talk. "Never disturb a sleeping child or a cooking egg," was one of his maxims.

"I knew that I should be happy here," said Mr. Langham. "I am."

Whenever he had a chance he gazed at Mary. It was her face in the row of six that had lured him out of all his habits and made him feel that the camp offered him a genuine chance for happiness. To find that she presided over the kitchen had filled his cup to the brim. But when he remembered that he was fat and fond of good things to eat and drink, his heart sank.

He determined that he would eat but three eggs. They were, however, prepared in a way that was quite new to him, and in the determined effort to discern the ingredients and the method he ate five.

"There is something very keen about your Adirondack air," he explained guiltily.

But Mary had warmed to him. Her heart and her reputation were involved in the *cuisine*. She knew that the better you feed people the more they love you. She was not revolted by Mr. Langham's appetite. She felt that even a canary of a man must have fallen before the temptation of those eggs.

They were her own invention. And chef had executed them to the very turn of perfection.

Almost from the moment of his arrival, then, Mr. Samuel Langham began to eat his way into the heart of the eldest Miss Darling.

In culinary matters a genuine intimacy sprang up between them. They exchanged ideas. They consulted. They compared menus. They mastered the contents of the late Mr. Darling's cellars.

Mr. Langham chose Lone House for his habitation. He liked the little balcony that thrust out over the lake between the two pine-trees. And by the time that his guests were due to arrive, he had established himself, almost, in the affections of the entire family.

"He may be greedy," said Arthur, "but he's the most courteous man that ever 'sat at meat among ladies'!"

"He's got the kindest heart," said Mary, "that ever beat."

VII

MR. LANGHAM'S five guests arrived somewhat noisily, smoking five long cigars.
Lee and Gay, watching the float from a point
of vantage, where they themselves were free from
observation, observed that three of the trout
fishermen were far older than they had led themselves to expect.

"That leaves only one for us," said Gay.

"Why ?"

"Can't you see from here that the fifth is an
Englishman ?"

"Yes," said Lee. "His clothes don't fit, and
yet he feels perfectly comfortable in them."

"It isn't so much the clothes," said Gay, "as
the face. The other faces are excited because
they have ridden fast in a fast boat, though they've
probably often done it before. Now he's probably
never been in a fast boat in his life till to-day,
and yet he looks thoroughly bored."

The Englishman without changing his expression made some remark to the other five. They
roared. The Englishman blushed, and looked
vaguely toward a dark-blue mountain that rose

with some grandeur beyond the farther shore of the lake.

"Do you suppose," said Lee, "that what he said was funny or just dumb?"

"I think it was funny," said Gay, "but purely accidental."

"I think I know the other youth," said Lee; "I think I have danced with him. Didn't Mr. Langham say there was a Renier among his guests?"

"H. L.," Gay assented.

"That's the one," Lee remembered. "Harry Larkins Renier. We have danced. If he doesn't remember, he shall be snubbed. I like the old guy with the Mark Twain hair."

"Don't you know *him?* I do. I have seen his picture often. He's the editor of the *Evening Star*. Won't Arthur be glad!"

"What's his name?"

"Walter Leyden O'Malley. He's the literary descendant of the great Dana. Don't talk to me, child; I know a great deal."

Gay endeavored to assume the look of an encyclopædia and failed.

"Mr. Langham," said Lee, "mentioned three other names, Alston, Pritchard, and Cox. Which do you suppose is which?"

The Seven Darlings

"I think that Pritchard is the very tall one who looks like a Kentucky colonel; Cox is the one with the very large face; of course, the Englishman is Alston."

"I don't."

"We can find out from Maud."

When the new arrivals, escorted by Arthur and Mr. Langham, had left the office, Lee and Gay hurried in to look at their signatures and to consult Maud as to identities.

The Kentucky-colonel-looking man proved to be Alston. Cox had the large face, and the Englishman—John Arthur Merrivale Pritchard, as was to be expected—wrote the best hand. Mr. O'Malley, the famous editor, wrote the worst. His signature looked as if it had been traced by an inky worm writhing in agony.

"Tell us at once," Gay demanded, "what they are like."

Maud regarded her frolicsome sisters with inscrutable eyes, and said:

"At first, you think that Mr. Cox is a heartless old cynic, but when you get to know him really well—I remember an instance that occurred in the early sixties——"

"Oh, dry up!" said Lee. "Are they nice and presentable, like fat old Sam Langham?"

The Seven Darlings

"The three old ones," said Maud, "made me think of three very young boys just loose from school. Messrs. Renier and Pritchard, however, seem more used to holidays. There is, however, a complication. All five wish to go fishing as soon as they can change into fishing clothes, and there aren't enough guides to go around."

"What's the trouble?" asked Gay eagerly.

"Bullard," Maud explained, "has sent word that his wife is having a baby, and Benton has gone up to Crotched Lake West to see if the ice is out of it. That leaves only three guides to go around. Benton oughtn't to have gone. Nobody told him to. But he once read the Declaration of Independence, and every now and then the feeling comes over him that he must act accordingly."

"But," exclaimed Lee, "what's the matter with Gay and me?"

"Nothing, I hope," said Maud; "you look well. I trust you feel well."

"We want to be guides," said Gay; "we want to be useful. Hitherto we've done nothing to help. Mary works like a slave in the kitchen; you here. Eve will never leave the laundry once the wash gets big. Phyllis has her garden, in which things will begin to grow by and by, but we —we have no excuse for existence—none whatever. Now, I could show Mr. Renier where the chances of taking fish are the best."

"No," said Lee firmly; "I ought to guide him. It's only fair. He once guided me—I've always remembered—bang into a couple who outweighed us two to one, and down we went."

"Mary will hardly approve of you youngsters going on long expeditions with strange young men," Maud was quite sure; "and, of course, Arthur won't."

Lee and Gay began to sulk.

At that moment Arthur came into the office.

"Halloo, you two !" he said. "Been looking for you, and even shouting. The fact is, we're short of guides, and Mary and I think——"

Lee and Gay burst into smiles.

"What did we tell you, Maud ? Of course, we will. There are no wiser guides in this part of the woods."

"That," said Arthur, "is a fact. The older men looked alarmed when I suggested that two of my sisters—you see, they've always had native-born woodsmen and even Indians——"

"Then," said Lee, "we are to have the guile-less youths. I speak for Renier."

"Meanie," said Gay.

"Lee ought to have first choice," said Arthur.

The Seven Darlings

"It's always been supposed that Lee is your senior by a matter of twenty minutes."

"True or not," said Gay, "she looks it. Then I'm to guide the Englishman."

"If you don't mind." Arthur regarded her, smiling. He couldn't help it. She was *so* pretty. "And I'd advise you not to be too eager to show off. Mr. Pritchard has hunted and fished more than all of us put together."

"That little pink-faced snip!" exclaimed Gay. "I'll sure see how much he knows."

Half an hour later she was rowing him leisurely in the direction of Placid Brook, and examining his somewhat remarkable outfit with wondering eyes. This was not difficult, since his own eyes, which were clear brown, and very shy, were very much occupied in looking over the contents of the large-tackle box.

"If you care to rig your rod," said Gay presently, "and cast about as we go, you might take something between here and the brook."

"Do you mean," he said, "that you merely throw about you at random, and that it is possible to take fish?"

"Of course," said she—"when they are rising."

"But then the best one could hope for," he drawled, "would be indiscriminate fish."

The Seven Darlings

"Just what do you mean by that?"

"Why!"—and this time he looked up and smiled very shyly—"if you were after elephant and came across a herd, would you pick out a bull with a fine pair of tusks, or would you fire indiscriminately into the thick of them, and perhaps bring down the merest baby?"

"I never heard of picking your fish," said Gay.

"Dear me," he commented, "then you have nearly a whole lifetime of delightful study before you!"

He unslung a pair of field-glasses, focussed them, and began to study the surface of the placid lake, not the far-off surface but the surface within twenty or thirty feet. Then he remarked:

"Your flies aren't greatly different from ours. I think we shall find something nearly right. One can never tell. The proclivities of trout and char differ somewhat. I have never taken char."

"You don't think you are after char now, do you?" exclaimed Gay. "Because, if so—this lake contains bass, trout, lake-trout, sunfish, shiners, and bullheads, but no char."

Pritchard smiled a little sadly and blushed. He hated to put people right.

"Your brook-trout," he said, "your *salmo fontinalis*, isn't a trout at all. He's a char."

59

The Seven Darlings

Gay put her back into the rowing with some tem-
per. She felt that the Englishman had insulted
the greatest of all American institutions. The repartee which sprang to her lips was somewhat feeble.

"If a trout is a char," she said angrily, "then
an onion is a fruit."

To her astonishment, Mr. Pritchard began to
laugh. He dropped everything and gave his
whole attention to it. He laughed till the tears
came and the delicate guide boat shook from
stem to stern. Presently the germ of his laughing
spread, and Gay came down with a sharp attack
of it herself. She stopped rowing. Two miles
off, a loon, that most exclusive laugher of the
North Woods, took fright, dove, and remained
under for ten minutes.

The young people in the guide boat looked at
each other through smarting tears.

"I am learning fast," said Gay, "that you count
your fish before you catch them, that trout are
char, and that Englishmen laugh at other people's
jokes."

She rowed on.

"Don't forget to tell me when you've chosen
your fish," she remarked.

"You shall help me choose," he said; "I insist.
I speak for a three-pounder."

The Seven Darlings

"The event of a lifetime!"

"Why, Miss Gay," he said, "it's all the event of a lifetime. The Camp, the ride in the motor-boat, the wonderful, wonderful breakfast, water teeming with fish, the woods, and the mountains —millions of years ago it was decreed that you and I should rock a boat with laughter in the midst of New Moon Lake. And yet you speak of a three-pounder as the event of a lifetime! My answer is a defiance. We shall take one *salmo fontinalis*—one wily char. He shall not weigh three pounds; he shall weigh a trifle more. Then we shall put up our tackle and go home to a merry dinner."

"Mr. Pritchard," said Gay, "I'll bet you any-thing you like that you don't take a trout—or a char, if you like—that will weigh three pounds or over. I'll bet you ten to one."

"Don't do that," he said; "it's an even shot. What will you bet?"

"I'll bet you my prospective dividends for the year," she said, "against——"

"My prospective title?"

He looked rather solemn, but laughter bubbled from Gay.

"It's a good sporting proposition," said Pritch-ard. "It's a very sound title—old, resonant—

The Seven Darlings

and unless you upset us and we drown, tolerably certain to be mine to pay—in case I lose."

"I don't bet blindly," said Gay. "What is the title?"

"I shall be the Earl of Merrivale," said he; "and if I fail this day to take a char weighing three pounds or over, you will be the Countess of Merrivale."

"Dear me!" said Gay, "who ever heard of so much depending on a mere fish? But I don't like my side of the bet. It's all so sudden. I don't know you well enough, and you're sure to lose."

"I'll take either end of the bet you don't like," said Mr. Pritchard gravely. "If I land the three-pounder, you become the countess; if I don't, I pay you the amount of your dividends for the year. Is that better?"

"Much," smiled Gay; "because, with the bet in this form, there is practically no danger that either of us will lose anything. My dividends probably won't amount to a row of pins, and you most certainly will not land so big a fish."

Meanwhile they had entered the mouth of Placid Brook. The surface was dimpling—rings became, spread, merged in one another, and were not. The fish were feeding.

The Seven Darlings

"Let us land in the meadow," said Mr. Pritchard, his brown eyes clear and sparkling, "and
spy upon the enemy."

"Are you going to leave your rod and things
in the boat?"

"For the present—until we have located our
fish."

They landed, and he advanced upon the brook
by a détour, stealthily, crouching, his field-glasses
at attention. Once he turned and spoke to Gay
in an authoritative whisper:

"Try not to show above the bushes."

VIII

THE sun was warm on the meadow, and although the bushes along its margin were leafless, the meadow itself had a greenish look, and the feel of the air was such that Gay, upon whom silence and invisibility had been enjoined, longed to dance in full sight of the trout and to sing at the top of her voice: "Oh, that we two were Maying!" Instead, she crouched humbly and in silence at Pritchard's side, while he studied the dimpling brook through his powerful field-glasses.

Gay had never seen red Indians except in Buffalo Bill's show, where it is made worth their while to be very noisy. But she had read her Cooper and her Ballantyne,

> "Ballantyne, the brave,
> And Cooper of the wood and wave,"

and she knew of the early Christian patience with which they are supposed to go about the business of hunting and fishing.

Pritchard, she observed, had a weather-red face and high cheek-bones. He was smooth-

The Seven Darlings

shaved. He wore no hat. But for his miraculously short-cut hair, his field-glasses, his suit of coarse Scotch wool, whose colors blended so well with the meadow upon which he crouched, he might have been an Indian. His head, the field-glasses, the hands which clasped them, moved—nothing else.

"Is it a bluff?" thought Gay. "Is he just posing, or is there something in it?"

Half an hour passed—three quarters. Gay was pale and grimly smiling. Her legs had gone to sleep. But she would not give in. If an Englishman could fish so patiently, why, so could she. She was fighting her own private battle of Bunker Hill—of New Orleans.

Pritchard lowered his glasses, handed them to Gay, and pointed up the brook and across, to where a triangular point of granite peered a few inches above the surface. Gay looked through the glasses, and Pritchard began to whisper in her ear:

"Northwest of that point of rock, about two feet—keep looking just there, and I'll try to tell you what to see."

"There's a fish feeding," she answered; "but he must be a baby, he just makes a bubble on the surface."

The Seven Darlings

"There are three types of insect floating over him," said Pritchard; "I don't know your American beasts by name, but there is a black, a brown, and a grayish spiderlike thing. He's taking the last. If you see one of the gray ones floating where he made his last bubble, watch it."

Gay presently discerned such an insect so floating, and watched it. It passed within a few inches of where the feeding trout had last risen and disappeared, and a tiny ring gently marked the spot where it had been sucked under. Gay saw a black insect pass over the fatal spot unscathed, then browns; and then, once more, a gray, very tiny in the body but with longish legs, approached and was engulfed.

"Now for the tackle box," Pritchard whispered.

They withdrew from the margin of the brook, Gay in that curious ecstasy, half joy, half sorrow, induced by sleepy legs. She lurched and almost fell. Pritchard caught her.

"Was the vigil too long?" he asked.

"I liked it," she said. "But my legs went to sleep and are just waking up. Tell me things. There were fish rising bold—jumping clean out —making the water boil. But you weren't interested in them."

"It was noticeable," said Pritchard, "and per-

The Seven Darlings

haps you noticed that one fish was feeding alone. He blew his little rings—without fear or hurry— none of the other fishes dared come anywhere near him. He lives in the vicinity of that pointed rock. The water there is probably deep and, in the depths, very cold. Who knows but a spring bubbles into a brook at the base of that rock? The fish lives there and rules the water around him for five or six yards. He is selfish, fat, and old. He feeds quietly because nobody dares dispute his food with him. He is the biggest fish in this reach of the brook. At least, he is the biggest that is feeding this morning. Now we know what kind of a fly he is taking. Probably I have a close imitation of it in my fly box. If not, we shall have to make one. Then we must try to throw it just above him—very lightly— float it into his range of vision, and when he sucks it into his mouth, strike—and if we are lucky we shall then proceed to take him."

Gay, passionately fond of woodcraft, listened with a kind of awe.

"But," she said, seeing an objection, "how do you know he weighs three pounds and over?"

"Frankly," said Pritchard, "I don't. I am gambling on *that*." He shot her a shy look. "Just hoping. I know that he is big. I believe

The Seven Darlings

we shall land him. I hope and pray that he weighs over three pounds."

Gay blushed and said nothing. She was beginning to think that Pritchard might land a three-pounder as well as not—and she had light-heartedly agreed, in that event, to become the Countess of Merrivale. Of course, the bet was mere nonsense. But suppose, by any fleeting chance, that Pritchard should not so regard it? What *should* she do? Suppose that Pritchard had fallen victim to a case of love at first sight? It would not, she was forced to admit (somewhat demurely), be the first instance in her own actual experience. There was a young man who had so fallen in love with her, and who, a week later, not knowing the difference—so exactly the triplets resembled each other—had proposed to Phyllis.

They drew the guide boat up onto the meadows and Pritchard, armed with a scoop-net of mesh as fine as mosquito-netting, leaned over the brook and caught one of the grayish flies that were tickling the appetite of the big trout.

This fly had a body no bigger than a gnat's.

Pritchard handed Gay a box of japanned tin. It was divided into compartments, and each compartment was half full of infinitesimal trout flies.

The Seven Darlings

They were so small that you had to use a pair of tweezers in handling them.

Pritchard spread his handkerchief on the grass, and Gay dumped the flies out on it and spread them for examination. And then, their heads very close together, they began to hunt for one which would match the live one that Pritchard had caught.

"But they're too small," Gay objected. "The hooks would pull right through a trout's lip."

"Not always," said Pritchard. "How about this one?"

"Too dark," said Gay.

"Here we are then—a match or not?"

The natural fly and the artificial placed side by side were wonderfully alike.

"They're as like as Lee and me," said Gay.

"Lee?"

"Three of us are triplets," she explained. "We look exactly alike—and we never forgive people who get us mixed up."

Pritchard abandoned all present thoughts of trout-fishing by scientific methods. He looked into her face with wonder.

"Do you mean to tell me," said he, "that there are two other D-D-Darlings exactly like you?"

"Exactly—a nose for a nose; an eye for an eye."

The Seven Darlings

"It isn't true," he proclaimed. "There is nobody in the whole world in the least like you."

"Some time," said Gay, "you will see the three of us in a row. We shall look inscrutable and say nothing. You will not be able to tell which of us went fishing with you and which stayed at home——"

" 'This little pig went to market,' " he began, and abruptly became serious. "Is that a challenge?"

"Yes," said Gay. "I fling down my gauntlet."

"And I," said Pritchard, "step forward and, in the face of all the world, lift it from the ground —and proclaim for all the world to hear that there is nobody like my lady—and that I am so prepared to prove at any place or time—come weal, come woe. Let the heavens fall!"

"If you know me from the others," Gay's eyes gleamed, "you will be the first strange young man that ever did, and I shall assign and appoint in the inmost shrines of memory a most special niche for you."

Pritchard bowed very humbly.

"That will not be necessary," he said. "If I land the three-pounder. In that case, I should be always with you."

"I wish," said Gay, "that you wouldn't refer

"They're as like as Lee and me," said Gay

so earnestly to a piece of nonsense. Upon repetition, a joke ceases to be a joke."

Pritchard looked troubled.

"I'm sorry," he said simply. "If it is the custom of the country to bet and then crawl, so be it. In Rome, I hasten to do as the Romans do. But I thought our bet was honorable and aboveboard. It seems it was just an—an Indian bet."

Gay flushed angrily.

"You shall not belittle anything American," she said. "It was a bet. I meant it. I stand by it. If you catch your big fish I marry you. And if I have to marry you, I will lead you such a dance——"

"You wouldn't have to," Pritchard put in gently, "you wouldn't have to lead me, I mean. If you and I were married, I'd just naturally dance—wouldn't I? When a man sorrows he weeps; when he rejoices he dances. It's all very simple and natural——"

He turned his face to the serene heavens, and, very gravely:

"Ah, Lord!" he said. "Vouchsafe to me, undeserving but hopeful, this day, a char—*salmo fontinalis*—to weigh a trifle over three pounds, for the sake of all that is best and sweetest in this best of all possible worlds."

The Seven Darlings

If his face or voice had had a suspicion of irreverence, Gay would have laughed. Instead, she found that she wanted to cry and that her heart was beating unquietly.

Mr. Pritchard dismissed sentiment from his mind, and with loving hands began to take a powerful split-bamboo rod from its case.

IX

GAY'S notion of scientific fishing might have been thus summed: Know just where to fish and use the lightest rod made. Her own trout-rod weighed two and a half ounces without the reel. Compared to it, Pritchard's was a coarse and heavy instrument. His weighed six ounces.

"You could land a salmon with that," said Gay scornfully.

"I have," said Pritchard. "It's a splendid rod. I doubt if you could break it."

"Doesn't give the fish much of a run for his money."

"But how about this, Miss Gay?"

He showed her a leader of finest water-blue catgut. It was nine feet long and tapered from the thickness of a human hair to that of a thread of spider-spinning. Gay's waning admiration glowed once more.

"That wouldn't hold a minnow," she said.

"We must see about that," he answered; "we must hope that it will hold a very large char."

The Seven Darlings

He reeled off eighty or ninety feet of line, and began to grease it with a white tallow.

"What's that stuff?" Gay asked.

"Red-deer fat."

"What for?"

"To make the line float. We're fishing with a dry-fly, you know."

Gay noticed that the line was tapered from very heavy to very fine.

"Why is that?" she asked.

"It throws better—especially in a wind. The heavy part will carry a fly out into half a gale."

He reeled in the line and made his leader fast to it with a swift, running hitch, and to the fine end of the leader he attached the fly which they had chosen. Upon this tiny and exquisite arrangement of fairy hook, gray silk, and feathers, he blew paraffin from a pocket atomizer that it might float and not become water-logged.

"Do we fish from the shore or the boat?" Gay asked.

"From this shore."

"You'll never reach there from this shore."

"Then I've misjudged the distance. Are you going to use the landing-net for me, in case it's necessary?"

The Seven Darlings

Gay caught up the net and once more followed his stealthy advance upon the brook.

Pritchard had one preliminary look through the field-glasses, straightened his bent back, turned to her with a sorrowing face, and spoke aloud.

"He's had enough," he said. "He's stopped feeding."

Gay burst out laughing.

"And our fishing is over for the day? This shall be said of you, Mr. Pritchard, that you are a merciful man. You are not what is called in this country a 'game hog.'"

"Thank you," he said gravely. "But if you think the fishing is over for the day, you don't know a dry-fly fisherman when you see one. We made rather a late start. See, most of the fish have stopped feeding. They won't begin again much before three. The big fellow will be a little later. He has had more than the others; he is older; his digestion is no longer like chain lightning; he will sleep sounder, and dream of the golden days of his youth when a char was a trout."

"*That*," said Gay, "is distinctly unkind. I have been snubbed enough for one day. Are we to stand here, then, till three or four o'clock, till his royal highness wakes up and calls for breakfast?"

"No," said Pritchard; "though I would do so gladly, if it were necessary, in order to take this particular fish——"

"You might kneel before your rod," said Gay, "like a knight watching his arms."

"To rise in the morning and do battle for his lady—I repeat I should do so gladly if it would help my chances in the slightest. But it wouldn't."

He rested his rod very carefully across two bushes.

"The thing for us to do," he went on, "is to have lunch. I've often heard of how comfortable you American guides can make the weary, wayworn wanderer at the very shortest notice."

"Is that a challenge?"

"It is an expression of faith."

Their eyes met, and even lingered.

"In that case," said Gay, "I shall do what I may. There is cold lunch in the boat, but the wayworn one shall bask in front of a fire and look upon his food when it is piping hot. Come!"

Gay rowed him out of the brook and along the shore of the lake for a couple of miles. She was on her mettle. She wished him to know that she was no lounger in woodcraft. She put her strong young back into the work of rowing, and the fragile guide boat flew. Her cheeks glowed, and her lips were parted in a smile, but secretly she was filled with dread. She knew that she had brought food, raw and cooked; she could see the head of her axe gleaming under the middle seat; she would trust Mary for having seen to it that there was pepper and salt; but whether in the pocket of the Norfolk jacket there were matches, she could not be sure. If she stopped rowing to look, the Englishman would think that she had stopped because she was tired. And if, later, it was found that she had come away without matches, he would laugh at her and her pretenses to being a "perfectly good guide."

She beached the boat upon the sand in a wooded cove, and before Pritchard could move had drawn it high and dry out of the water. Then she laughed aloud, and would not tell him why. She had discovered in the right-hand pocket of her coat two boxes of safety-matches, and in the left pocket three.

"Don't," said Gay, "this is my job."

She lifted the boat easily and carried it into the woods. Pritchard had wished to help. She laid the boat upon soft moss at the side of a narrow, mounting trail, slung the package of lunch upon her shoulders, and caught up her axe.

"Don't I help at all?" asked Pritchard.

"You are weary and wayworn," said Gay, "and I suppose I ought to carry you, too. But I can't. Can you follow? It's not far."

A quarter of a mile up the hillside, between virgin pines which made one think bitterly of what the whole mountains might be if the science of forestry had been imported a little earlier in the century, the steep and stony trail ended in an open space, gravelly and abounding in huge bowlders, upon which the sun shone warm and bright. In the midst of the place was a spring, black and slowly bubbling. At the base of one great rock, a deep rift in whose face made a natural chimney, were traces of former fires.

"Wait here," commanded Gay.

Her axe sounded in a thicket, and she emerged presently staggering under a load of balsam. She spread it in two great, fragrant mats. Then once more she went forth with her axe and returned with fire-wood.

Pritchard, a wistful expression in his eyes, studied her goings and her comings, and listened as to music, to the sharp, true ringing of her axe.

The Seven Darlings

"By Jove," said he to himself, "that isn't perspiration on her forehead—it's honest sweat!"

In spite of the bright sunshine, the heat of the fire was wonderfully welcome, and began to bring out the strong, delicious aroma of the balsam. Gay sat upon her heels before the fire and cooked. There was a sound of boiling and bubbling. The fragrance of coffee mingled with the balsam and floated heavenward. During the swift preparation of lunch they hardly spoke. Twice Pritchard begged to help and was twice refused.

She spread a cloth between the mats of balsam upon one of which Pritchard reclined, and she laid out hot plates and bright silver with demure precision.

"Miss Gay," he said very earnestly, "I came to chuckle; I thought that at least you would burn the chicken and get smoke in your eyes, but I remain to worship the deity of woodcraft. An Indian could not do more swiftly or so well."

Gay swelled a little. She had worked very hard; nothing had gone wrong, so far. She was not in the least ashamed of herself. But her greatest triumph was to come.

Uncas, the chipmunk, had that morning gone for a stroll in the forest. He had the spring fever.

The Seven Darlings

He had crossed Placid Brook, by a fallen log; he had climbed trees, hunted for last year's nuts, and fought battles of repartee with other chipmunks. About lunch time, thinking to return to Arthur and recount the tale of his wanderings, he smelled a smell of cooking and heard a sound of voices, one of which was familiar to him. He climbed a bowlder overlooking the clearing, and began to scold. Gay and Pritchard looked up.

"My word!" said Pritchard, "what a bold little beggar."

Now, to Gay, the figure of Uncas, well larded with regular meals, was not to be confounded with the slim little stripes of the spring woods. She knew him at once, and she spoke nonchalantly to Pritchard.

"If you're a great deal in the woods," she said, "you scrape acquaintance with many of the inhabitants. That little pig and I are old friends. You embarrass him a little. He doesn't know you. If you weren't here, he'd come right into my lap and beg."

Pritchard looked at her gravely.

"Truly?" he said.

"I think he will anyway," said Gay, and she made sounds to Uncas which reassured him and brought him presently on a tearing run for her lap. Here, when he had been fed, he yawned, stretched himself, and fell asleep.

"Mowgli's sister!" said Pritchard reverently. "Child, are there the scars of wolves' teeth on your wrists and ankles?"

"No, octogenarian," said Gay; "there aren't any marks of any kind. What time is it?"

"It is half-past two."

"Then you shall smoke a cigarette, while I wash dishes."

She slid the complaining Uncas from her lap to the ground.

"Unfortunately," said Pritchard, "I didn't bring a cigarette."

"And you've been dying for a smoke all this time? Why don't you ask the guide for what you want?"

"Have you such a thing?"

"I have."

"But you—you yourself don't—do you?" He looked troubled.

"No," said Gay. "But my father was always forgetting his, and it made him so miserable I got into the habit of carrying a full case years ago whenever we went on expeditions. He used to be so surprised and delighted. Sometimes I think he used to forget his on purpose, so that I could have the triumph of producing mine."

Pritchard smoked at ease. Gay "washed up." Uncas, roused once more from slumber by the call of one of his kind, shook himself and trotted off into the forest.

Gay, scouring a pan, was beginning to feel that she had known Pritchard a long time. She had made him comfortable, cared for him in the wild woods, and the knowledge warmed her heart.

Pritchard was saying to himself:

"We like the same sort of things—why not each other?"

"Miss Gay," he said aloud.

"What?"

"In case I land the three-pounder and over, I think I ought to tell you that I'm not very rich, and I know you aren't. Would that matter to you? I've just about enough," he went on tantalizingly, "to take a girl on ripping good trips into central Africa or Australia, but I can't keep any great state in England—Merrivale isn't a show place, you know—just a few grouse and pheasants and things, and pretty good fishin'."

"However much," said Gay, "I may regret my *bet*, there was nothing Indian about it. I'm sure that you are a clean, upright young man.

The Seven Darlings

I'm a decent sort of girl, though I say it that shouldn't. We might do worse. I've heard that love-matches aren't always what they are cracked up to be. And I'm quite sure that I want to go to Africa and hunt big game."

"Thank you," said Pritchard humbly. "And at least there would be love on one side."

"Nonsense," said Gay briskly. "I'm ready, if you are."

Pritchard jumped to his feet and threw away his cigarette.

"Now," he said, "that you've proved everything, *won't* you let me help?"

Gay refused him doubtfully, and then with a burst of generosity:

"Why, yes," she said, "and, by the way, Mr. Pritchard, there was no magic about the chipmunk. He's one my brother trained. He lives at The Camp, and he was just out for a stroll and happened in on us. I don't want you to find out that I'm a fraud from any one—but me."

X

THE big trout was once more feeding. And
Pritchard began to cast his diminutive fly
up-stream and across. But he cast and got out
line by a system that was new to Gay. He did
not "whip" the brook; he whipped the air above
it. He never allowed his fly to touch the water
but drew it back sharply, and, at the same time,
reeled out more line with his left hand, when it
had fallen to within an inch or two of the surface.
His casts, straight as a rifle-shot, lengthened, and
reached out toward the bowlder point near which
the big trout was feeding, until he was throwing,
and with consummate ease, a line longer than
Gay had ever seen thrown.

"It's beautiful," she whispered. "Will you
teach me?"

"Of course," he answered.

His fly hovered just above the ring which the
trout had just made. Pritchard lengthened his
line a foot, and cast again and again, with no
further change but of an inch or two in direction.

"There's a little current," he explained. "If

The Seven Darlings

we dropped the fly into the middle of the ring, it would float just over his tail and he wouldn't see it. He's looking up-stream, whence his blessings flow. The fly must float straight down at him, dragging its leader, and not dragged by it."

All the while he talked, he continued casting with compact, forceful strokes of his right wrist and forearm. At last, his judgment being satisfied by the hovering position attained by fly and leader, he relaxed his grip of the rod; the fly fell upon the water like thistle-down, floated five or six inches, and was sucked under by the big trout.

Pritchard struck hard.

There was a second's pause, while the big trout, pained and surprised, tried to gather his scattered wits. Three quarters of Pritchard's line floated loosely across the brook, but the leader and the fly remained under, and Pritchard knew that he had hooked his fish.

Then, and it was sudden—like an explosion—the whole length of floating line disappeared, and the tip of Pritchard's powerful rod was dragged under after it.

The reel screamed.

"It's a whale!" shouted Gay, forgetting how much depended upon the size of the fish, "a whale!"

The Seven Darlings

The time for stealthy movements and talk in whispers was over. Gay laughed, shouted, exhorted, while Pritchard, his lips parted, his cheeks flushed, gayly fought the great fish.

"Go easy; go easy!" cried Gay. "That hook will never hold him."

But Pritchard knew his implements, and fished with a kind of joyous, strong fury.

"When you hang 'em," he exulted, "land 'em."

The trout was a great noble potentate of those waters. Years ago he had abandoned the stealthy ways of lesser fish. He came into the middle of the brook where the water is deep and there is freedom from weeds and sunken timber, and then up and down and across and across, with blind, furious rushes he fought his fight.

It was the strong man without science against the strong man who knows how to box. The steady, furious rushes, snubbed and controlled, became jerky and spasmodic; in a roar and swirl of water the king trout showed his gleaming and enormous back; a second later the sunset colors of his side and the white of his belly. Inch by inch, swollen by impotent fury, galvanically struggling and rushing, he followed the drag of the leader toward the beach, where, ankle-deep

The Seven Darlings

in the water, Gay crouched with the landing-net.

She trembled from head to foot as a well-bred pointer trembles when he has found a covey of quail and holds them in control, waiting for his master to walk in upon them.

The big trout, still fighting, turning, and raging, came toward the mouth of the half-submerged net.

"How big is he, Miss Gay?"

The voice was cool and steady.

"He's five pounds if he's an ounce," her voice trembled. "He's the biggest trout that ever swam."

"He *isn't* a trout," said Pritchard; "he's a char."

If Gay could have seen Pritchard's face, she would have been struck for the first time by a sort of serene beauty that pervaded some of its expressions. The smile which he turned upon her crouching figure had in it a something almost angelic.

"Bring him a little nearer," she cried, "just a little."

"You're sure he weighs more than three pounds?"

"Sure — sure — don't talk, land him, land him——"

The Seven Darlings

For answer Pritchard heaved strongly upward upon his rod and lifted the mighty fish clear of the water. One titanic convulsion of tortured muscles, and what was to be expected happened. The leader broke a few inches from the trout's lip, and he returned splashing to his native element, swam off slowly, just under the surface, then dove deep, and was seen no more.

"Oh!" cried Gay. "Why *did* you? Why *did* you?"

She had forgotten everything but the fact that the most splendid of all trout had been lost.

"Why did you?" she cried again.

"Because," he said serenely and gently, smiling into her grieved and flushed face, "I wouldn't have you as the payment of a bet. I will have you as a gift or not at all."

They returned to The Camp, Pritchard rowing.

"I owe you your prospective dividends for the year," he said. "If they are large, I shall have to give you my note and pay as I can."

She did not answer.

"I think you are angry with me," he said. "I'd give more than a penny for your thoughts."

"I was thinking," said she, "that you are very good at fishing, but that the art of rowing

The Seven Darlings

an Adirondack guide boat has been left out of you."

"Truly," he said, "was that what you were thinking?"

"No," she said; "I was thinking other things. I was thinking that I ought to go down on my knees and thank you for breaking the leader. You see, I'd made up my mind to keep my word. And, well, of course, it's a great escape for me."

"Why? Was the prospect of marrying me so awful?"

"The prospect of marrying a man who would rather lose a five-pound fish than marry me—was awful."

Pritchard stopped rowing, and his laughter went abroad over the quiet lake until presently Gay's forehead smoothed and, after a prelude of dimples, she joined gayly in.

When Pritchard could speak, he said:

"You don't really think that, do you?"

"I don't know what I think," said Gay. "I'm just horrid and cross and spoiled. Don't let's talk about it any more."

"But I said," said he, "I said 'As a bet, no; but as a gift'—oh, with what rapture and delight!"

The Seven Darlings

"Do you mean that?" She looked him in the face with level eyes.

Once more he stopped rowing.

"I love you," he said, "with my whole heart and soul."

"Don't," said Gay, "don't spoil a day that, for all its ups and downs, has been a good day, a day that, on the whole, I've loved—and let's hurry, please, because I stood in the water and it was icy."

After that Pritchard rowed with heroic force and determination; he lacked, however, the knack which overlapping oar handles demand, and at every fifteenth or sixteenth stroke knocked a piece of "bark" from his knuckles.

Smarting with pain, he smiled gently at her from time to time.

"Will you guide me to-morrow?"

"To-morrow," she said, "there will be enough real guides to go around."

"You really are, aren't you?" he said.

"What?"

"Angry with me."

"Oh, no—I think—that what you said—what you said—was a foolish thing to say. If I came to you with my sisters Lee and Phyllis, you wouldn't know which of the three I was, and yet —you said—you said——"

The Seven Darlings

"It isn't a question of words—it's a question of feeling. Do you really think I shouldn't know you from your sisters?"

"I am sure of it," said Gay.

"But if you weren't?"

"Then I should still think that you had tried to be foolish but I shouldn't be angry."

"How," said Pritchard, his eyes twinkling, "shall I convince the girl I love—that I know her by sight?"

Gay laughed. The idea seemed rather comical to her.

"To-night," she said, "when you have dined, walk down to the dock alone. One of us three will come to you and say: 'Too bad we didn't have better luck.' And you won't know if she's Lee or Phyllis or me."

.   .   .   .

Pritchard smoked upon the dock in the light of an arc-lamp. A vision, smiling and rosy, swept out of the darkness, and said:

"Too bad we didn't have better luck!"

"I beg your pardon," said Pritchard, "you're not Miss Gay, but I haven't had the pleasure of being presented to Miss Lee or Miss Phyllis."

The vision chuckled and beat a swift, giggling

The Seven Darlings

retreat to a dark spot among the pines, where other giggles awaited her.

A second vision came.

"Too bad we didn't have better luck!"

Pritchard smiled gravely into the vision's eyes, and said in so low a voice that only she could hear:

"Bad luck? I have learned to love you with all my heart and soul."

Silence. An answering whisper.

"How did you know me?"

"How? Because my heart says here is the only girl in all the world—see how different, how more beautiful and gentle she is than all other girls."

"But I'm not Gay—I'm Phyllis."

"If you are Phyllis," he whispered, "then you never were Gay."

She laughed softly.

"I *am* Gay."

"Why tell me? I know. Am I forgiven?"

"There is nothing," she said swiftly, "to forgive," and she fled swiftly.

To her sisters waiting among the pines she gave explanation.

"Of course, he knew me."

"How?"

The Seven Darlings

"Why, he said there couldn't be any doubt; he said I was so very much better-looking than any sister of mine could possibly be."

Forthwith Lee pinioned Gay's arms and Phyllis pulled her ears for her.

Mr. Pritchard paced the dock, offering rings of Cuban incense to the stars.

.   .   .   .

From Play House came the sounds which men make when they play cards and do not care whether they win or lose.

Maud was in her office, adding a column of figures which the grocer had sent in. The triplets, linked arm in arm, joined her. Arthur came, and Eve and Mary.

They agreed that they were very tired and ready for bed.

"It's going to be a success, anyway," said Mary. "That seems certain."

"We must have the plumber up," said Eve; "the laundry boiler has sprung a leak. Who's that in your pocket, Arthur?"

"Uncas. He came in exhausted after a long day in the woods. Something unusual happened to him. I know, because he tried so very hard to tell me all about it just before he went to sleep, and of course he couldn't quite make me understand. I think he was trying to warn me of something—trying to tell me to keep my eyes peeled."

The family laughed. Arthur was always so absurd about his pets. All laughed except Gay. She, in a dark corner, like the rose in the poem, blushed unseen.

XI

WHEN their week was up, Mr. Langham's guests, Messrs. O'Malley, Alston, and Cox, felt obliged to go where income called them. Renier, however, who had only been at work a year, decided that he did not like his job, and would try for another in the fall. Lee delivered herself of the stern opinion that a rolling stone gathers no moss, and Renier answered that his late uncle had been a fair-to-middling moss gatherer, and that to have more than one such in a given family was a sign of low tastes. "I have a little money of my own," he said darkly, "and, what's more, I have a little hunch." To his face Lee upbraided him for his lack of ambition and his lack of elegance, but behind his back she smiled secretly. She was well pleased with herself. It had only taken him three days to get so that he knew her when he saw her, and for a young man of average intellect and eyesight that was almost a record.

The triplets were not only as like as three lovely vases cast in the same mould but it amused

The Seven Darlings

them to dress alike, without so much as the differentiation of a ribbon, and to imitate each other's little tricks of speech and gesture. It was even possible for them to fool their own brother at times when he happened to be a little absent-minded.

Every day Renier fished for many hours, and always the guide who handled his boat and showed him where to throw his flies was Lee.

"They're only children," said Mary, "and I think they're getting altogether too chummy."

Arthur did not answer, and for the very good reason that Mary's words were not addressed to him, nor were they addressed to Maud or Eve. Indeed, at the moment, these three were sound asleep in their beds. It was to that plumper and earlier bird, Mr. Samuel Langham, that Mary had spoken. The end of a kitchen table, set with blue-and-white dishes and cups that steamed, fragrantly separated them. They had formed a habit of breakfasting together in the kitchen, and it had not taken Mary long to discover that Sam Langham's good judgment was not confined to eatables and drinkables. She consulted him about all sorts of things. She felt as if she had known him (and trusted him) all her life.

"Renier," he said, "is one of the few really

The Seven Darlings

eligible young men I know. That is why I asked him up here. I don't mean that my intention was match-making, but when I saw your picture in the advertisement, I said to myself: 'The Inn is no place for attractive scalawags. Any man that goes there on my invitation must be sound, morally and financially.' Young Renier is as innocent of anything evil as Miss Lee herself. If they take a fancy to each other—of course it's none of my business, but, my dear Miss Darling —why not ?"

"Coffee ?"

"Thanks."

"An egg ?"

"Please."

Mary was very tactful. She never said: "*Some more* coffee ?" She never said: "*Another* egg ?"

"Some people," said Mr. Langham, smiling happily, "might say that *we* were getting too chummy."

"Suppose," said Mary, "that somebody did say just that ?"

"I should reply," said Mr. Langham thoughtfully, "that of the few really eligible men that I know, I myself am, on the whole, the most eligible."

Mary laughed.

97

The Seven Darlings

"Construe," she said.

"In the first place," he continued, "and naming my qualifications in the order of their importance, I don't ever remember to have spoken a cross word to anybody; secondly, unless I have paved a primrose path to ultimate indigestion and gout, there is nothing in my past life to warrant mention. To be more explicit, I am not in a position to be troubled by—er—'old agitations of myrtle and roses'; third, something tells me that in a time of supreme need it would be possible for me to go to work; and, fourth, I have plenty of money—really plenty of money."

Mary smiled almost tenderly.

"I can't help feeling," she said, "that I, too, am a safe proposition. I am twenty-nine. My wild oats have never sprouted. I think we may conclude that they were never sown. The Inn was my idea—mostly, though I say it that shouldn't. And The Inn is going to be a success. We could fill every room we've got five times—at our own prices."

"I pronounce your bill of health sound," said Mr. Langham. "Let us continue to be chummy."

"Coffee?"

"Thanks."

Whatever chance there may have been for

"I said to myself: 'The Inn is no place for attractive scalawags'"

The Seven Darlings

Gay and Pritchard to get "too chummy"—and no one will deny that they had made an excellent start—was promptly knocked in the head by Arthur. It so happened that, in a desperately unguarded moment, when Arthur happened to be present, Pritchard mentioned that he had spent a whole winter in the city of Peking. The name startled Arthur as might the apparition of a ghost.

"Which winter?" he asked. "I mean, what year?"

Pritchard said what year, and added, "Why do you ask?"

Arthur had not meant to ask. He began a long blush, seeing which Gay turned swift heels and escaped upon a suddenly ejaculated pretext.

"Why," said Arthur lamely, "I knew some people who were in Peking that winter—that's all."

"Then," said Pritchard, "we have mutual friends. I knew every foreigner in Peking. There weren't many."

Although Arthur had gotten the better of his blush, he felt that Pritchard was eying him rather narrowly.

"They," said Arthur, "were a Mr. and Mrs. Waring."

The Seven Darlings

"I hope," said Pritchard, "that *he* wasn't a friend of yours."

"He was not," said Arthur, "but she was. I was very fond of her."

"Nobody," said Pritchard, "could help being fond of her. But Waring was an old brute. One hated him. He wouldn't let her call her soul her own. He was always snubbing her. We used to call her the 'girl with the dry eyes.'"

"Why?" asked Arthur.

"It's a Chinese idea," said Pritchard. "Every woman is supposed to have just so many tears to shed. When these are all gone, why, then, no matter what sorrows come to her, she has no way of relieving them."

Arthur could not conceal his agitation. And Pritchard looked away. He wished to escape. He thought that he could be happier with Gay than with her brother. But Arthur, agitation or no agitation, was determined to find out all that the young Englishman could tell him about the Warings. He began to ask innumerable questions: "What sort of a house did they live in?" "How do Christians amuse themselves in the Chinese capital?" "Did Mrs. Waring ride?" "What were some of her friends like?" etc., etc. There was no escaping him. He fastened himself to Pritchard as a drowning man to a straw. And his appetite for Peking news became insatiable. Pritchard surrendered gracefully. He went with Arthur on canoe trips and mountain climbs; at night he smoked with him in the open camp. And, in the end, Arthur gave him his whole confidence; so that, much as Pritchard wished to climb mountains and go on canoe trips with Gay, he was touched, interested, and gratified, and then all at once he found himself liking Arthur as much as any man he had ever known.

"There is something wonderfully fine about your brother," he said to Gay. "At first I thought he was a queer stick, with his pets and his secret haunts in the woods, and his unutterable contempt for anything mean or worldly. We ought to dress him up in proof armor and send him forth upon the quest of some grail or other."

"Grails," said Gay, "and auks are extinct."

"Grails extinct!" exclaimed Pritchard. He was horrified.

"Why, my dear Miss Gay, if ever the world offered opportunities to belted knights without fear and without reproach, it's now."

"I suppose," said she, "that Arthur has told you all about his—his mix-up."

Pritchard nodded gravely.

The Seven Darlings

"Is that the quest he ought to ride on?"

"No—it won't do for Arthur. He might be accused of self-interest. That should be a matter to be redressed by a brother knight."

"Or a divorce court."

"Miss Gay!"

"I don't think it's nice for one's brother to be in love with a married woman."

"It isn't," said Pritchard gravely, "for him. It's hell."

"*We*," said Gay, "never knew her."

"She's not much older than you," said Pritchard. "If I'd never seen you, I'd say that she was the prettiest girl I'd ever seen. But she's gentler and meeker than even you'd be in her boots. She isn't self-reliant and able."

"You talk as if you'd been in love with her yourself."

"I? I thought I was talking as if I was in love with you."

"Looks like it, don't it?" said she. "Spending all your time with a girl's brother."

"Not doing what you most want to do," said Pritchard, "is sometimes thought knightly."

"Do you know," she said critically, "sometimes I think you really like me a lot. And sometimes I think that I really like you. The funny

The Seven Darlings

thing is that it never seems to happen to both of us at the same time. There's Arthur looking for you. Do me a favor—shake him and come for a tramp with me."

"I can't," said Pritchard simply. "I've promised. But to-morrow——"

"*Certainly not,*" said she.

XII

WARM weather and the real opening of the season arrived at the same time. The Camp hummed with the activities and the voices of people. And it became possible for the Darlings to withdraw a little into their shells and lead more of a family life. As Maud said:

"When there were more proprietors than guests, we simply had to sail in and give the guests a good time. But now that the business is in full blast, we mustn't be amateurs any more."

Langham, Renier, and the future Earl of Merrivale remained, of course, upon their well-established footing of companionship, but the Darlings began to play their parts of innkeepers with the utmost seriousness and to fight shy of any social advances from the ranks of their guests.

Indeed, for the real heads of the family, Mary, Maud, and Eve, there was serious work to be done. For, to keep thirty or forty exigent and extravagant people well fed, well laundered, well served, and well amused is no frisky skirmish

The Seven Darlings

but a morning-to-night battle, a constant looking ahead, a steady drain upon the patience and invention.

In Sam Langham Mary found an invaluable ally. He knew how to live, and could guess to a nicety the "inner man" of another. Nor did he stop at advice. Being a celebrated *bon viveur* he went subtly among the guests and praised the machinery of whose completed product they were the consumers and the beneficiaries. He knew of no place, he confided, up and down the whole world, where, for a sum of money, you got exactly what you wanted without asking for it.

"Take me for an example," he would say. "I have never before been able to get along without my valet. Here he would be a superfluity. I am 'done,' you may say, better than I have ever been able to do myself. And I know what I'm talking about. What! You think the prices are really rather high. Think what you are getting, man—think!"

Among the new guests was a young man from Boston by the name of Herring. He had written that he was convalescing from typhoid fever and that his doctor had prescribed Adirondack air.

Renier knew Herring slightly and vouched for him.

The Seven Darlings

"They're good people," he said, "his branch of the Herring family—the 'red Herrings' they are called locally—if we may speak of Boston as a 'locality'—he's the reddest of them and the most showy. If there's anything he hasn't tried, he has to try it. He isn't good at things. But he does them. He's the fellow that went to the Barren Lands with a niblick. What, you never heard of that stunt? He was playing in foursome at Myopia. He got bunkered. He hit the sand a prodigious blow and the ball never moved. His partner said: 'Never mind, Syd, you hit hard enough to kill a musk-ox.'

"'Did I?' said Herring, much interested, 'but I never heard of killing a musk-ox with a niblick. Has it ever been done? Are there any authorities one might consult?'

"His partner assured him that 'it' had never been done. Herring said that was enough for him. The charm of Herring is that he never smiles; he's deadly serious—or pretends to be. When they had holed out at the eighteenth, Herring took his niblick and said: 'Well, so long. I'm off to the Barren Lands.'

"They bet him there and then that he would neither go to the Barren Lands nor kill a musk-ox when he got there. He took their bets, which

The Seven Darlings

were large. And he went to the Barren Lands, armed only with his niblick and a camera. But he didn't kill a musk-ox. He said they came right up to be photographed, and he hadn't the heart to strike. He brought back plenty enough pictures to prove where he'd been, but no musk-ox. He aimed at one tentatively but at the last moment held his hand. 'He remembered suddenly,' he said, 'that he had never killed anything, and didn't propose to begin.' So he came home and paid one bet and pocketed the other. He can't shoot; he can't fish; he can't row. He's a perfect dub, but he's got the soul of a Columbus."

"Something tells me," said Pritchard, "that I shall like him."

Herring, having arrived and registered and been shown his rooms, was not thereafter seen to speak to anybody for two whole days. As a matter of fact, though, he held some conversation with Renier, whom he had met before.

"It's just Boston," Renier explained. "They're the best people in the world—when—well, not when you get to know them but when they get to know you. Give him time and he will blossom."

"He looks like a blossom already," said Lee. "He looks at a little distance like a gigantic plant of scarlet salvia, or a small maple-tree in October."

Upon the third day Mr. Herring came out of his shell, as had been prophesied. He went about asking guests and guides, with almost plaintive seriousness, questions which they were unable to answer. He began to make friends with Pritchard and Langham. He solemnly presented Arthur with a baseball that had figured in a Yale-Harvard game. Then he got himself introduced to Lee.

"You guide, don't you?" he said.

"I have guided," she said, "but I don't. It was only in the beginning of things when there weren't enough real guides to go around. But, surely you don't need a guide. You've been to the Barren Lands and all sorts of wild places. You ought to be a first-class woodsman."

"I thought I'd like to go fishing to-morrow," he said. "It's very disappointing. I've looked forward all my life to being guided by a young girl, and when I saw you, I said, if this isn't she, this is her living image."

"You shall have Bullard," said Lee. "He knows all the best places."

Herring complained to Arthur. "Your sisters," he said, "are said to be the best guides in the

The Seven Darlings

Adirondacks, but they won't take me out. How is a fellow to convalesce from typhoid if people aren't unfailingly kind to him?"

Arthur laughed, and said that he didn't know.

"Let me guide you," he offered.

"No," said Herring, "it isn't that I want to be guided. It's that I want the experience of being guided by a girl. I want to lean back and be rowed."

Herring walked in the woods and came upon Phyllis's garden, with Phyllis in the midst of it.

"Halloo again!" he said.

Now it so happened that he had never seen Phyllis before.

She straightened from a frame of baby lettuce and smiled. She loved bright colors, and his flaming hair was becoming to her garden.

"Halloo again!" she said.

"Have you changed your mind?" he asked.

She sparred for time and enlightenment and said:

"It's against all the rules."

"We could," said he, "start so early that nobody would know. I have often gotten up at five."

"So have I," said Phyllis wistfully.

"We could be back before breakfast."

The Seven Darlings

Phyllis appeared to think the matter over.

"Of course," he said, "you said you wouldn't. But if girls didn't change their minds, they wouldn't be girls."

"That," said Phyllis, "is perfectly true."

To herself she said:

"He's asked Lee or Gay to guide him, and thinks he's asked me."

Now, Phyllis was not good with oars or fishing-tackle, but she liked Herring's hair and the fact that he never smiled. Furthermore, she believed that, if the worst came to the worst, she could find some of the places where people sometimes took trout.

"I have never," said Herring, "been guided by a young girl."

"What, never!" exclaimed Phyllis.

"Never," he said. "And I am sure that it would work wonders for me."

"Such as?"

"It might lead me to take an interest in gardening. I have always hoped that I should some day."

"People," thought Phyllis, "interested in gardening are rare—especially beautiful young gentlemen with flaming hair. Here is my chance to slaughter two birds with one stone."

The Seven Darlings

"You'll swear not to tell?" she exhorted.

"Yes," he said, "but not here. Soon. When I am alone." He did not smile.

"Then," she said, "be at the float at five-thirty sharp."

That night she sought out Lee and Gay.

"Such a joke," she said. "I've promised to guide Mr. Herring—to-morrow at five-thirty, but he thinks that it's one of you two who has promised. Now, as I don't row or fish, one of you will have to take my place for the credit of the family."

But her sisters were laughing in their sleeves.

"My dear girl," said Gay, "why the dickens didn't you tell us sooner? We also have made positive engagements at five-thirty to-morrow morning."

"What engagements?" exclaimed Phyllis.

Gay leaned close and whispered confidentially.

"We've made positive engagements," she said, "to sleep till breakfast time."

XIII

IN an athletic generation Phyllis was an
anachronism. She was the sort of girl one's
great-grandmother was, only better-looking—one's
great-grandmother, if there is any truth in oil
and canvas, having been neatly and roundly
turned out of a peg of wood. Phyllis played no
game well, unless gardening is a game. She liked
to embroider and to write long letters in a wonderfully neat hand. She disliked intensely the roaring of firearms and the diabolic flopping of fresh-
caught fish. She was one of those people who
never look at a sunset or a moonrise or a flower
without actually seeing them, and yet, withal, her
sisters Lee and Gay looked upon her with a certain awe and respect. She was so strong in the
wrists and fingers that she could hold them when
they were rambunctious. And she was only
afraid of things that aren't in the least dangerous.
"No," they said, "she can't fish and shoot and
row and play tennis and dive and swim under
water, but she's the best dancer in the family—
probably in the world—and the best sport."

The Seven Darlings

Phyllis was, in truth, a good sport, or else she was more attracted by Mr. Herring's *Salvia-splendens* hair than she would have cared to admit. Whatever the cause, she met him at the float the next morning at five-thirty, prepared to guide him or perish in the attempt. She wore a short blue skirt and a long white sweater of Shetland wool. It weighed about an ounce. She wore white tennis shoes and an immense pair of well-oiled gardening gloves. At least she would put off blistering her hands as long as possible.

Phyllis, to be exact, was five minutes early for her appointment. This gave her time to get a boat into the water without displaying awkwardness to any one but herself—also, to slip the oars over the thole-pins and to accustom herself to the idea of handling them. She had taken coaching the night before from Lee and Gay, sitting on a bearskin rug in front of the fire, and swaying rhythmically forward and back.

As Herring was no fisherman, her sisters advised her to row very slowly. "Tell him," they said, "that a boat rushing through water alarms fish more than anything in the world."

She told him when he was seated in the stern of the boat facing her.

"You mustn't mind going very slow," she said.

The Seven Darlings

"The fish in this part of the Adirondacks are noted for their sensitiveness in general and their acute sense of hearing in particular. Why, if I were to row as fast as I can"—there must have been a twinkle in her eyes—"trout miles away would be frightened out of their skins," and she added mentally, "and I should upset this horribly wabbly boat into the bargain."

They proceeded at a snail's pace, Phyllis dabbing the water gingerly with her oars, with something of that caution and repulsion with which one turns over a dead snake with a stick—to see if it is dead.

The grips of guide-boat oars overlap. And your hands follow rather than accompany each other from catch to finish, and from finish to catch. If you are careless, or not to the stroke born or trained, you occasionally knock little chunks of skin and flesh from your knuckles.

Herring watched Phyllis's gentle and restrained efforts with inscrutable eyes.

"I never could understand," he said, "how you fellows manage to row at all with that sort of an outfit. At Harvard they only give you one oar and let you take both hands to it, and then you can't row. At least, I couldn't. They put me right out of the boat. They said I caught

The Seven Darlings

crabs. As a matter of fact, I didn't. All I did
was to sit there, and every now and then the
handle of my oar banged me across the solar
plexus."

"We're not going far, you know," said Phyllis
(and she mastered the desire to laugh). "Hadn't
you—ah—um—better put your rod together?"

"Oh, I can do that!" said Herring. "You
begin with the big piece and you stick the next-
sized piece into that, and so on. And I know
how to put the reel on, because the man in the
store showed me, and I know how to run the line
through the rings."

"Well," said Phyllis, "that's more than half
the battle."

"And," Herring continued, "he showed me
how to tie on the what-you-may-call-it and the
flies."

"Good!" said Phyllis.

"And, of course," he concluded, "I've forgotten."

Now, Phyllis had been shown how to tie flies
to a leader only the night before, and she, also,
had forgotten.

"There are," she said, "a great many fetiches
among anglers. Among them are knots. Now,
in my experience, almost any knot that will stand

will do. The important thing is to choose the right flies."

As to this, she had also received instruction, but with better results, since it was an entirely feminine affair of colored silks and feathers.

"I will tell you which flies to use," she said.

"And," said he, "you will also have to show me how to cast."

"What!" she exclaimed, and stopped rowing. "You don't know how to cast?"

"No," he said, "I don't. I'm a dub. Didn't you know that?"

"But," she protested, "I can't teach you in a morning"—and she added mentally—"or in a whole lifetime, for that matter."

It was not more than a mile across the mouth of a deep bay to the brook in which they had elected to fish. With no wind to object, the most dabbily propelled guide boat travels with considerable speed, and before Herring had managed to tie the flies which Phyllis had selected to his leader (with any kind of a knot) they were among the snaggy shallows of the brook's mouth.

The brook was known locally as Swamp Brook, its shores for a mile or more being boggy and treacherous. Fishermen who liked to land occasionally and cast from terra firma avoided it.

The Seven Darlings

Phyllis had selected it solely because it was the nearest brook to the camp which contained trout. If she had remembered how full it was of snags, and how easily guide boats are turned turtle, she would have selected some other brook, even, if necessary, at the "Back of beyond." It had been easy enough to propel the boat across the open waters of the lake, but to guide it clear of snags and around right-angle bends, especially when the genius of rowing demands that eyes look astern rather than ahead, was beyond her powers. The boat ran into snags, poked its nose into boggy banks, turned half over, righted, rushed on, and stopped again with rude bumps.

Herring, that fatalistic young Bostonian, began to take an interest in his fate. His flies trailed in the water behind him. His eyes never left Phyllis's face. His handsome mouth was as near to smiling as it ever got.

"Do you," he said presently, "swim as well as you row?"

She stopped rowing; she laughed right out. "Just about," she said.

"Good," he said seriously, "because I'm a dub at it, and in case of an upset, I look to you."

"The truth," said Phyllis, "is that there's no place to swim to. It's all swamp in here."

The Seven Darlings

"True," said Herring; "we would have to cling to the boat and call upon Heaven to aid us."

One of Herring's flies, trailing in the water, proved, at this moment, overwhelmingly attractive to a young and unsophisticated trout.

Herring shouted with the triumph of a schoolboy, "I've got one," and sprang to his feet.

"Please sit down!" said Phyllis. "We almost went that time."

"So we did," said Herring.

He sat down, and they almost "went" again.

"Now," said Phyllis, "play him."

"Play him?" said Herring. "Watch me." And he began to pull strongly upon the fish.

The fish was young and weak. Herring's tackle was new and strong. The fish dangled in mid-air over the middle of the boat.

"Sorry," said Herring, "I can't reach him. Take him off, please."

It has been said that Phyllis was a good sport. If there was one thing she hated and feared more than another, it was a live fish. She reached forward; her gloved hand almost closed upon it; it gave a convulsive flop; Phyllis squeaked like a mouse, threw her weight to one side, and the boat quietly upset.

The sportsmen came to the surface streaming.

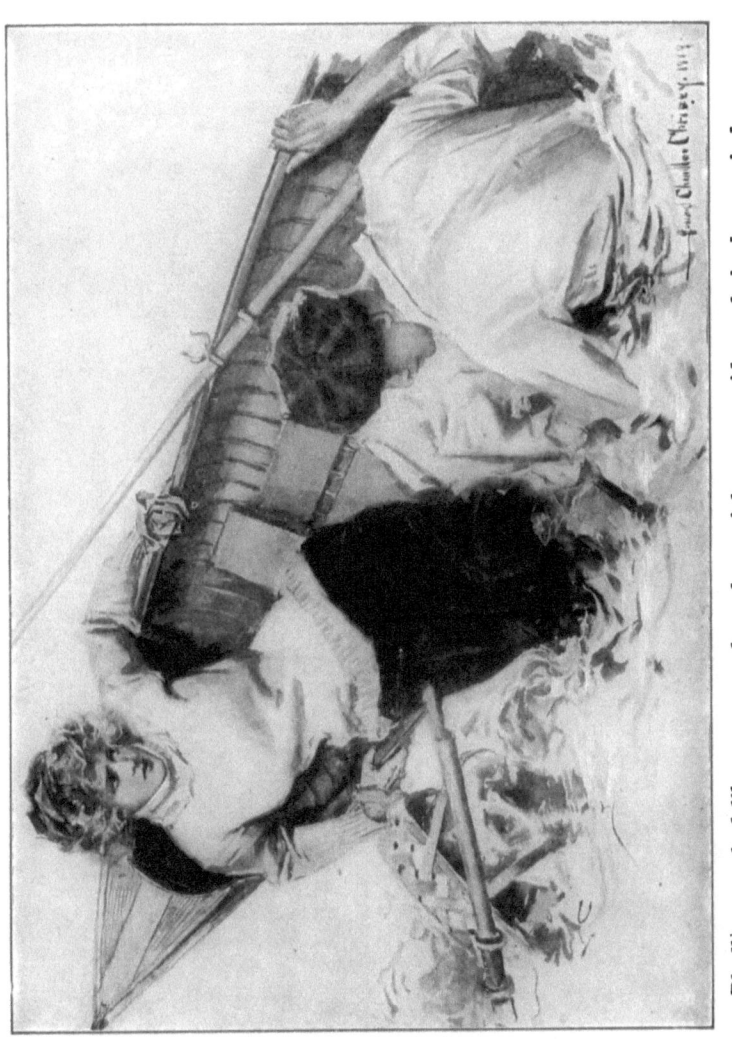

Phyllis squeaked like a mouse, threw her weight to one side, and the boat quietly upset

The Seven Darlings

"I can touch bottom," said Herring politely; "can you?"

"Yes," she said, "but my feet are sinking into it—" She tore them loose and swam. Herring did likewise. And they clung to the boat.

"I hope you'll forgive me," said Phyllis. "I never rowed a boat before and I never could stand live fish."

"It was my fault," said Herring. "Something told me to lean the opposite from the way you leaned. But it told me too late. The truth is I don't know how to behave in a boat. Well, you are still guide. It's up to you."

"What is up to me?"

"A plan of some sort," said he, "to get us out of this."

"Oh, no," she said, "it's up to you."

"My plan," he said, "would be to get back into the boat and row home. It seems feasible, and even easy. But appearances are deceptive. I think I'd rather walk. What has happened here might happen out on the middle of the lake."

"What you don't realize," said Phyllis, "is that we're in the midst of an impassable swamp."

"Impassable?"

"Well, no one's ever crossed it except in winter."

"What—no one!"

He was immensely interested.

"Do you know," he went on confidentially, "the only things that I'm good at are things for which there are no precedents—things that nobody has ever done before. That's why I'm so fond of doing unusual things. Now, you say that this swamp has never been crossed? Enough said. You and I will cross it. We *will* do it. Are you game?"

"It seems," said Phyllis, "merely a question of when and where we drown. So I'm game. Your teeth are chattering."

"Thank you," said Herring. "But no harm will come to them. They are very strong."

"I hope," said Phyllis, "that when I come out of the water you won't look at me. I shall be a sight."

"A comrade in trouble," said Herring, "is never a sight."

"I am so ashamed," said Phyllis.

"What of?"

"Of being such a fool."

"You're a good sport," said Herring. "That's what you are."

By dint of violent kicking and paddling with their free hands they managed to propel the guide boat from the centre of the brook to a firm-looking clump of reeds and alder roots which formed a tiny peninsula from that shore which was toward The Camp. Covered with slime and mud they dragged themselves out of the water and stood balancing upon the alder roots to recover their breath.

"We must each take an oar," said Herring. "We can make little bridges with them. And we must keep working hard so as to get warm. We shall live to write a brochure about this: 'From Clump to Clump, or Mudfoots in the Adirondacks.'"

Between that clump on which they had found a footing and the next was ten feet of water.

Herring crossed seven feet of it with one heavy jump, fell on his face, caught two handfuls of viburnum stems, and once more dragged himself out of water.

"Now then," he called, "float the oars over to me." And when Phyllis had done this: "Now you come. The main thing in crossing swamps is to keep flat instead of up and down. Jump for it—fall forward—and I'll get your hands!"

Once more they stood side by side precariously balancing.

"The moment," said Herring, "that you begin to feel bored, tell me."

The Seven Darlings

"Why?"

"So that I can encourage you. I will tell you that you are doing something that has never been done before. And that will make you feel fine and dandy. What we are doing is just as hard as finding the North Pole, only there isn't going to be so much of it. Now then, in negotiating this next sheet of water——"

And so they proceeded until the sun was high in the heavens and until it was low.

XIV

TO attempt the dangerous passage of a swamp when they might have returned to camp in the guide boat was undoubtedly a most imbecile decision. And if Phyllis had not been thoroughly flustered by the upset, which was all her fault, she never would have consented to it. As for Herring's voice in the matter, it was that which the young man always gave when there was a question of adventure. He didn't get around mountains by the valley road. He climbed over them. He had not in his whole being a suspicion of what is dangerous. He had never been afraid of anything. He probably never would be. He would have enjoyed leading half a dozen forlorn hopes every morning before breakfast.

"We were idiots," said Phyllis, "to leave the boat."

"We can't go back to it now," said Herring. "We don't know the way."

"Your voice sounds as if you were glad of it."

"I am. I was dreadfully afraid you'd decide

against crossing this swamp. I'd set my heart on it."

"It isn't I," said Phyllis, "that's against our crossing this swamp. It's the swamp."

"The main thing," said Herring, with satisfaction (physically he was almost exhausted), "is that here we are safe and sound. We don't know where 'here' is, but it's with us, it won't run away. When we've rested we shall go on, taking 'here' with us. Wherever we go is 'here.' Think of that!"

"I wish I could think of something else," said Phyllis, "but I can't. I'm almost dead."

"You are doing something that no girl has ever done before, not even your sisters, those princesses of fortune. Years from now, when you begin, 'Once when I happened to be crossing the Swamp with a young fellow named Herring—' they will have to sit silent and listen."

"If you weren't so cheerful," said Phyllis, "I should have begun to cry an hour ago. Do you really think this is fun?"

"Do I think it's fun? To be in a scrape—not to know when or how we are going to get out of it? You bet I think it's fun."

"People have died," said Phyllis, "having just this sort of fun. Suppose we can't get out?"

The Seven Darlings

"You mean to-day? Perhaps we can't. Perhaps not to-morrow. Perhaps we shall have to learn how to live in a swamp. A month of the life we've led for the last few hours might turn us into amphibians. That would be intensely novel and interesting. But, of course, when winter comes and the place freezes over we can march right out and take up our orthodox lives where we left off. Listen!"

"What?"

"I think I hear webs growing between my fingers and toes."

Phyllis laughed so that the partially dried mud on her face cracked.

"What," she said, "are we going to eat this side of winter? What are we going to eat now?"

His face expressed immense concern.

"What? You are hungry? Allow me!"

He produced from his inside pocket a very large cake of sweet chocolate, wrapped in several thicknesses of oiled silk.

"My one contribution," he said, "to the science of woodcraft."

Phyllis ate and was refreshed. Afterward she washed all the mud from her face. Herring watched the progress of the ablution with much interest.

The Seven Darlings

"Wonderful!" he said presently.

"What is wonderful?" she asked, not without anticipation of a compliment.

"Wonderful to find that something which is generally accepted as true—is true. To see it proved before your eyes."

"What do you mean?"

"I mean," he said, "that I never before actually saw a girl wash her face. I've seen 'em when they said they were going to. I've seen 'em when they said they just had. But now I know."

"If you weren't quite mad," said Phyllis, "you'd be very exasperating. Here am I, frightened half to death, cold and miserable, and dreadfully worried to think how worried my family must be, and there are you, almost too tired to stand, actually delighted with yourself, because you're in trouble and because for the first time in your life you've seen a girl wash her face. Can't you be serious about anything?"

"Not about a half-drowned girl taking the trouble to wash her face," he said.

"You," said she, "would look much better if you washed yours."

"But," he said, "we'll be covered with mud again before we've gone fifty yards."

"Because you are going into a coal mine to-morrow," said Phyllis, "is no reason why you shouldn't be clean to-day."

"True," said Herring, and he washed his face.

.   .   .   .

At breakfast that morning Pritchard received the following cablegram:

Come home and shake hands. I'm off.   M.

Greatly moved, he carried it to Gay, and without comment put it in her hand.

"Who is M?" she asked.

"My uncle, the Earl of Merrivale."

"What does *I'm off* mean?"

"It means," said Pritchard, "that they've given him up, and he wants to make friends. He never liked my father or me."

"It means," said Gay generously, "that you are going away?"

"Yes," he said, "at once. But it means more. It means that I've got to find out if I'm—to come back some time?"

"Of course, you are to come back," she said.

Words rose swiftly to Pritchard's lips and came no further. Indeed, he appeared to swallow them.

The Seven Darlings

"And I'm glad you are going to make friends with your uncle," said Gay.

"There'll be such lots of young men here when the season opens," said Pritchard.

"Judging by applications," said Gay, "we shall be swamped with gentlemen of all ages."

Pritchard's melancholy only deepened. "Will you come as far as Carrytown in the *Streak?*" he asked.

She nodded, and said she would because she had some shopping to do.

During that short, exhilarating rush across the lake, and afterward walking up and down on the board platform by the side of the waiting train, he tried his best to ring a little sentiment out of her, but failed utterly.

The locomotive whistled, and the conductor came out of the village drug-store, staggering slightly.

"I've left all my dry-fly tackle," said Pritchard. "Will *you* take care of it for me?"

"With pleasure," said Gay.

"I'd like you to use it. It's a lovely rod to throw line."

"All aboard!"

"I'd like to bring you out some rods and things. May I?"

The Seven Darlings

"You bet you may!" exclaimed Gay.

Pritchard sighed. The train creaked, jolted, moved forward, stopped, jerked, and moved forward again. Pritchard waited until the rear steps of the rear car were about to pass.

"Good-by, Miss Gay!"

They shook hands firmly, and Pritchard swung himself onto the moving train. Gay, walking rapidly and presently breaking into a trot, accompanied him as far as the end of the platform. She wanted to say something that would please him very much without encouraging him too much.

"Looks as if I was after you!" she said.

Pritchard's whole soul was in his eyes. And there was a large lump in his throat. Suddenly Gay reached the end of the long platform and stopped running. The train was now going quite fast for an Adirondack train. The distance between them widened rapidly.

"Wish you weren't going," called Gay.

And she saw Pritchard reach suddenly upward and pull the rope by which trains are stopped in emergencies. While the train was stopping and the train hands were trying to find out who had stopped it and why, Pritchard calmly alighted and returned to where Gay was standing.

The Seven Darlings

"I just had to look at you once more—close,"
he said; "you never can tell what will happen in
this world. I may never see you again, and the
thought is killing me. Think of that once in a
while, please."

He bent swiftly, caught her hand in his, kissed
it, and was gone. Or, if not exactly gone, she saw
him no more, because of suddenly blinding
tears.

When she reached The Camp, Arthur was at
the float to meet her.

"Phyllis and Herring haven't come back," he
said. "Lee says they went fishing. Do you
know where they went?"

"I don't. And they ought to have been back
hours ago."

"Yes," said Arthur, "and we're all starting
out to look for them. Care to come with me?"

"Yes," she said; "I've got to do *something*."

Something in her voice took his mind from the
more imminent matter.

"What's wrong, Gay?"

She shook her head.

"Nothing. Let's start. If Phyl rowed, they
must have gone to the nearest possible fishing
grounds."

At this moment Sam Langham came puffing

The Seven Darlings

down from Cook House. He was dressed in white flannels and carried a revolver.

"It's to signal with," he explained. "I'm going to try Loon Brook, because it's the only brook I know when I see it."

"Bullard's gone to Loon Brook."

"Pshaw—can't I ever be of any use!"

"Good Lord," said Gay, "look!"

There came around the nearest bend a man rowing one guide boat and towing another, which was empty. Arthur called to him in a loud, hoarse voice:

"Where'd you find that boat?"

"Up Swamp Brook," came the answer.

Arthur and Gay went gray as ashes.

"Who's to tell Mary?" said Arthur presently.

Then Sam Langham spoke.

"If you don't mind," he said, "I think I will."

An hour later the entire male population of The Camp was dragging Swamp Brook for what they so dreaded to find.

XV

IT wasn't all discouragement. For now and then it seemed as if the swamp was going to have a shore of dry land. At such times Herring would exclaim:

"There you see! It had never been done before, and now it's been done, and we've done it."

And then it would seem to Phyllis as if a great weight of fear and anxiety had been lifted from her.

But the shore of the swamp always turned out to be an illusion. Once Herring, firmly situated as he believed, went suddenly through a crust of sphagnum moss and was immersed to the armpits. For some moments he struggled grimly to extricate himself, and only sank the deeper. Then he turned to Phyllis a face whimsical in spite of its gravity and pallor, and said: "If you have never saved a man's life, now is your chance. I'm afraid I can't get out without help."

It was then that her phenomenally strong little hands and wrists stood them both in good stead. The arches of her feet against a submerged root of white cedar, she so pulled and tugged, and exhorted Herring to struggle free, that at last he came out of that pocket quagmire and lay exhausted in the ooze at her feet.

He was incased from neck to foot in a smooth coating of brown slime. Presently he rolled over on his back and looked up at her.

"There you see!" he said. "You'd never saved a man's life before, and now you've done it. Please accept my sincere expressions of envy and gratitude— Why, you're crying!"

She was not only crying, but she was showing symptoms of incipient hysteria. "An old-fashioned girl," thought Herring, "like Great-grandmother Saltonstall." He raised himself to a sitting position just in time to slide an arm around her waist as, the hysteria now well under way, she sat down beside him and began to wave her hands up and down like a polite baby saying good-by to some one.

"One new thing under the sun after another," thought Herring. "Never had arm round hysterical girl's waist before. Got it there now. When you need *her*, she takes a good brace and pulls for all she's worth. When she needs *you*, she seats herself on six inches of water and yells. Just like Great-grandmother Saltonstall." Aloud he kept saying: "That's right! Greatest relief in the world! Go to it!" And his arm tightened about her with extraordinary tenderness.

Her hysterics ended as suddenly as they had begun. And then she wasted a valuable half-hour apologizing for having had them; Herring protesting all the while that he had enjoyed them just as much as she had, and that they had done him a world of good. And then they had to stop talking because their teeth began to chatter so hard that they simply couldn't keep on. Herring stuttered something about, "Exercise is what a body needs," and they rose to their feet and fought their way through a dense grove of arborvitæ.

"The stealthy Indian goes through such places without making a sound," said Herring.

"Or getting his moccasins wet," said Phyllis. "Oh!" And she sank to the waist.

"Never mind," said Herring, "it will be dark before long. And when we have no choice of where to step, maybe we'll have better luck."

"It will *have* to be dark very soon," said Phyllis, "if we have any more of our clothes taken away from us by the brambles."

"That's a new idea!" exclaimed Herring.

The Seven Darlings

"Young couple starve to death in the woods because modesty forbids them to join their friends in the open. The head-line might be: 'Stripped by Brambles,' or 'The Two Bares.'"

He was so pleased with his joke that he had to lean against a tree. The laughing set him to coughing, and Phyllis beat him methodically between the shoulders.

Herring still refused to be serious. In helping Phyllis over the bad places, he performed prodigies of misapplied strength and made prodigious puns. And he said that never in his life had he been in such a delightful scrape.

Once, while they were resting, Phyllis said:

"All you seem to think of is the fun you're having. Most men would be thinking about the anxiety they were causing others and about the miseries of their companion."

"But," he protested, "you are enjoying yourself too. You don't think you are, but you are. It's your philosophy that is wrong. You like to live too much in the present. I like to lay by stores of delightful memories against rainy days. The worse you feel now, the more you'll enjoy remembering how you felt—some evening, soon —your back against soft cushions and the soles of your feet toward the fire."

The Seven Darlings

"Ugh!" shuddered Phyllis. "Don't talk about fires. Oh, dear!"

"What's wrong *now!*"

"I'm so stiff I don't think I can take another step. We oughtn't to have rested so long."

But she did take another step, and would have fallen heavily if Herring had not caught her. A moment later she lost a shoe in the ooze, and wasted much precious daylight in vain efforts to locate and recover it.

"Sit down on that root," commanded Herring. And she obeyed. He knelt before her, lifted her wet, muddy little stockinged foot and set it on his knee.

"What size, please, miss?" he asked, giving an excellent imitation of a somewhat officious salesman.

"I don't know; I have them made," said Phyllis wearily, but trying her best to smile.

"Something in this style?" suggested Herring. He had secretly removed one of his own shoes, and handling it with a kind of comic reverence, as if the soggy, muddy thing was a precious work of art, he presented it to her attention.

And then Phyllis smiled without even trying and then laughed.

136

The Seven Darlings

"I said a *shoe*," she said, "not a travelling bath-tub."

But he slipped that great shoe over her little foot, and so bound it to her ankle with his handkerchief and necktie that it promised to stay on.

"But you?" she said.

"Luck is with me to-day," said Herring. "Anybody can walk through an impassable swamp, but few are given the opportunity to hop. General Sherman should have thought of that. It would have showed the Confederates just what he thought of them if instead of marching through Georgia he had hopped."

And he pursued this new train of thought for some time. He improvised words to old tunes, and sang them at the top of his lungs: "As we were hopping through Georgia." And last and worst he sang: "There'll be a hop time in the old town to-night." And when he had occasion to address Phyllis directly, he no longer called her Miss Darling, but "Goody Two Shoes." He said that his own name was not Mr. Herring but Mr. Hopper, and that he was a famous cotillon leader.

But even he became a little quiet when the light began to fail, and a little serious.

"Whatever happens," he said, "it will be a great comfort to you to realize that it's entirely my fault. On the other hand, if we had gotten back into that boat, we might have been drowned long before this."

A little later Phyllis said: "I'm about all in. It's too dark to see. I——"

"Couldn't have chosen a better camping site myself," said Herring humbly. "First thing to think of is the water-supply—and fuel. Now, here the fuel grows right out of the water——"

"We haven't any matches."

"Yes, we have; but they are wet and won't light."

"We'll die of cold before morning," said Phyllis; "there's no use pretending we won't."

"On the contrary. Now is the time to pretend all sorts of things. Did you ever try to make a fire by rubbing two sticks together?"

"Never."

"Well, try it. It will make you warmer than the fire would. Afterward we will play 'Paddy cake, Paddy cake,' and 'Bean Porridge hot.'"

"Do men in danger always carry on the way you do?" asked Phyllis.

"Always," he answered.

"I can understand trying to be funny during a cavalry charge, or while falling off a cliff," said Phyllis, "but not while slowly and miserably congealing."

The Seven Darlings

"You are not a Bostonian," said Herring. "Half the inhabitants of that municipality freeze to death and the others burn."

"I've stayed in Boston," said Phyllis, "and the only difference that I could see between it and other places was that the people were more agreeable and things were done in better taste. And what gardens!"

"Ever seen the Arboretum?"

"Have I?"

"In lilac time?"

"Mm!"

She was on her favorite topic. She forgot that she was cold, wet, miserable, and a frightful anxiety to her family.

"But why be an innkeeper?" asked Herring. "Why not set up as a landscape-gardener?"

"I don't know enough. But I've often thought ——"

"I've got five hundred acres outside of Boston that I'd like to turn you loose on."

"You speak as if I were a goat."

"The first thing to do is to drain the swamps. Now, I'll make you a proposition. I can't put it in writing, because it's too dark to see and I have no writing materials, but there is nothing fishy about us Herrings. You to landscape my place

for me, cause a suitable house to be built, and so
forth; I to pay you a thousand dollars a month,
and a five per cent commission on the total ex-
penditure."

"And what might *that* amount to?"

"What you please," said Herring politely.

"Who says Bostonians are cold?" exclaimed
Phyllis. And there began to float through her head
lovely visions of landscapes of her own making.

"You're still joking, aren't you?" she said
after a while.

"I don't know landscapes well enough to joke
about them," he said.

"But I can't design a house!"

"Oh, you will have architects to do that part.
You just pick the general type."

"What kind of a house do you want?"

"It depends on what kind of a house *you* want."

"Oh, dear," she exclaimed, "what fun it would
be!"

"Will you do it?"

She was tempted beyond her strength.

"Yes," she said, and began to talk with ir-
responsible delight and enthusiasm.

"Ah," thought Herring to himself, "find out
what really interests a girl and she'll forget all
her troubles."

The Seven Darlings

It began suddenly to grow light.

"Good heavens!" exclaimed Phyllis. "The woods must be on fire! Oh, the poor trees!"

"It isn't fire," said Herring, "it's the moon— 'Queen and huntress, chaste and fair—goddess excellently bright'—was ever such luck! I hoped we were going to stand here cosily all night talking about marigolds and cowslips and wall-papers, and now it's our duty to move on. Come, Goody Two Shoes, Policeman Moon has told us to move on. I shall never forget this spot. And I shan't ever be able to find it again."

They toiled forward a little way, and lo! upon a sudden, they came to firm and rocky land that sloped abruptly upward from the swamp. They climbed for several hundred feet and came out upon a bare hilltop, from which could be seen billows of forest and one great horn of Half Moon Lake, silver in the moonlight.

"Why, it isn't a mile to camp," said Phyllis. She swayed a little, tottered, rocked backward and then forward, and fell against Herring's breast in a dead faint.

In a few moments she came to and found that she was being carried in strong arms. It was a novel, delicious, and restful sensation— one which it seemed immensely sensible to prolong. She did not, then, immediately open her eyes.

She heard a voice cheerful, but very much out of breath, murmuring over her:

"New experience. Never carried girl before. Experience worth repeating. Like 'em old-fashioned—like Great-grandmother Saltonstall. Like 'em to faint."

A few minutes later, "Where am I?" said Phyllis.

"In my arms," said Herring phlegmatically, as if that was one of her habitual residing places.

"Put me down, please."

"I hear," said he, "and I obey with extreme reluctance. I made a bet with myself that I could carry you all the way. And now I shall never know. Feel better?"

"Mm," she said, and "What a nuisance I've been all through! But it was pretty bad, some of it, wasn't it?"

"Already you are beginning to take pleasure in remembering. What did I tell you? Don't be frightened. I am going to shout."

He shouted in a voice of thunder, and before the echo came back to them another voice, loud and excited, rose in the forest. And they heard smashings and crashings, as a wild bull tearing

through brittle bushes. And presently Sam
Langham burst out of the thicket with a shower
of twigs and pine-needles.

His delight was not to be measured in words.
He apostrophized himself.

"Good old Sam!" he said. "He knew you
weren't drowned in the brook. He knew it
would be just like Herring to want to cross that
swamp. As soon as I heard somebody say that
it was impassable, I said: 'Where is the other side?
That's the place to look for them.' But why
didn't you make more noise?"

"Oh," said Herring, "we were so busy talking
and exploring and doing things that had never
been done before that it never occurred to us to
shout."

"Herring," said Langham sternly, "you have
the makings of a hero, but not, I am afraid, of a
woodsman."

"Well, we're safe enough now," said Herring.
"Excuse me a moment——"

"Excuse you! What?"

"It's very silly—been sick you know—over-
exertion—think better faint and get it over with."

Langham knelt and lifted Herring's head.

"You lift his feet," he said to Phyllis, "send
the blood to his heart ; bring him to."

The Seven Darlings

Herring began to come out of his faint.

"This young man," said Langham, "may be something of an ass, but he's got sand."

"He carried me a long way," said Phyllis, the tears racing down her cheeks; "and he's only just over typhoid, and he never stopped being cheerful and gallant, and he *isn't* an ass!"

Herring came to, but was not able to stand. He had kept up as long as he had to, and now there was no more strength in him.

Phyllis accepted the loan of Langham's coat.

"I'll stay with him," she said, "while you go for help."

The moment Langham's back was turned she spread the coat over Herring.

"*Please—don't!*" he said.

"You be quiet," said she sharply. "How do you feel?"

"Pretty well used up, thank you. Hope you'll 'scuse me for this collapse. Shan't happen again. Lucky thing you and I don't both collapse same moment."

A faint moan was wrung from him. She touched his cheek with her hand. It was hot as fire. She was an old-fashioned girl, and the instinct of nursing was strong in her.

She was an old-fashioned girl. There had

The Seven Darlings

almost always been a young man in her life about whom, for a while, she wove more or less intensely romantic fancies. They came; they went. But almost always there was one.

She raised her lovely face and looked at the moon, and made an unspoken confession. There had always been one. Well, now there was another!

XVI

WHEN the real season opened, you might have thought that the whole venture was Mr. Sam Langham's and that he had risked the whole of his money in it. Without being officious, he had words of anxious advice for the Darlings, severally and collectively. His early breakfasts in Smoke House with Mary, the chef beaming upon the efficient and friendly pair, lost something of their free and easy social quality, and became opportunities for the gravest discussions of ways and means.

The opening day would see every spare room in the place occupied—by a man. To Mary it seemed a little curious that so few women, so few families, and so many bachelors had applied for rooms. But to Sam Langham the reasons for this were clear and definite.

"It was the picture in the first issues of your advertisement that did it. I only compliment and felicitate you when I say that every bachelor who saw that picture must have made up his mind to come here if he possibly could. And that

The Seven Darlings

every woman who saw it must have felt that she could spend a happier summer somewhere else. Now, if you had circulated a picture of half a dozen men, each as good-looking as your brother Arthur, the results would have been just the opposite."

"Women aren't such idiots about other women's looks as you think they are," said Mary.

"I didn't say they were idiots; I intimated that they were sensible. The prettiest woman at a summer resort always has a good time—not the best, necessarily, but very good. Now, no woman could look at that picture of you and your sisters and expect to be considered the prettiest woman *here*. Could she, Chef?"

Chef laughed a loud, scornful, defiant, gesticulant, Gallic laugh. His good-natured features focussed into a scathing Parisian sneer; he turned a delicate omelette over in the air and said, "Lala!"

"There are," continued Mr. Langham, "only half a dozen women in the world who can compare in looks with you and your sisters. There's the Princess Oducalchi—your mother. There's the Countess of Kingston, Mrs. Waring, Miss Virginia Clark—but these merely compare. They don't compete."

The Seven Darlings

Mr. Langham tried to look very sly and wicked, and he sang in a humming voice: "Oh, to be a Mussulman, now that spring is here."

"Coffee?" said Mary.

"Please."

"Well," said she, as she poured, "the whys and wherefores don't matter. It's to be a bachelor resort—that seems definitely settled. But I think we had better send the triplets away. I don't want the Pritchard and Herring episodes repeated while my nerves are in this present state. And there's Lee—if she isn't leading Renier into one folly after another, I don't know what she is doing. They seem to think that keeping an inn is a mere excuse for flirtation."

"Don't send them away," said Langham. "If you sent those three girls to a place where there weren't any men at all—they'd flirt with their shadows. Better have 'em flirting where you can watch 'em than where you can't. And besides—are you quite sure that the Pritchard and Herring episodes were mere flirtations? Day before yesterday I came upon Miss Gay by accident; she was practising casting."

"That's how she spends half her time."

"But she was practising with Pritchard's rod! Yesterday I came upon her in the same place——"

The Seven Darlings

"By accident?" smiled Mary.

"By design," he said honestly. "And this time she wasn't casting. She had the rod lying across her knees, and her eyes were turned dreamily toward the bluest and most distant mountaintop."

"'Why do you look at that mountain?' I said.

"'Because it's blue, too,' said she.

"'And what makes you blue?' I asked.

"'The same cause that makes the mountain blue,' said she.

"'Hum,' said I. 'Then it must be distance.'

"'Something like that,' she said. 'I sometimes think I'm the most distant person in the world.'

"'You're probably not the only person who thinks that!' said I.

"And she said, 'No? Really?' And that was all I could get out of her. Except that, just as I was walking away, I heard a sharp whistling sound and my cap—my new plaid cap—was suddenly tweaked from the top of my head and hung in a tree. She must have practised a lot with that rod of Pritchard's. It was a beautiful cast——"

"She might have put your eye out!" exclaimed Mary.

The Seven Darlings

"She hung the apple of my eye in a tree," said he dolefully. "You know that one with the green and brown? And last night it rained."

"I hope she expressed sorrow," said Mary.

"She was going to, but I got laughing and then she did."

"What a dear you are!" exclaimed Mary. "And so you think she's making herself mournful over Mr. Pritchard? And what are the reasons for thinking that Phyllis is serious about Mr. Herring?"

"He's sent for blue-prints of his property outside Boston, and they are busy with plans for landscaping it. Narrow escape that! I didn't let on; but the second day I thought he was a goner. I did."

Mary sighed.

"We might just as well have called it a matrimonial agency in the first place instead of an inn."

Mr. Langham rose reluctantly.

"I have an engagement with Miss Maud," he explained.

The faintest ripple of disappointment flitted across Mary's forehead.

"I've promised to help her with her books," said he. "Some of the journal entries puzzle her;

"'Why do you look at that mountain?' I said. 'Because it's blue, too,' said she"

The Seven Darlings

and she has an idea that The Inn ought to have more capital. And we are going into that, too."

"I hope," said Mary, "that you aren't going to lend us money without consulting me."

Chef was in a distant corner, quite out of ear-shot. And Mr. Langham, emboldened by one of the most delicious breakfasts he had ever eaten, shot an arch glance at Miss Darling.

"I wouldn't consult you about lending money," he said; "I wouldn't consult you about giving money. But any time you'll let me consult you about *sharing* money——"

Panic overtook him, and he turned and fled. But upon Mary's brow was no longer any ripple of disappointment—only the unbroken alabaster of smooth serenity. She reached for the house-hold keys and said to herself:

"Maud is a steady girl—even if the rest of us aren't."

She caught a glimpse of herself in the bottom of a highly polished copper utensil and couldn't help being pleased with what she saw.

On the way 'to the office Mr. Langham fell in with Arthur. This one, Uncas scolding and chatting upon his shoulder, was starting off for a day's botanizing—or dreaming maybe.

"Arthur—one moment, please," said Langham. "As the head of the family I want to consult you about something."

"Yes?" said Arthur sweetly. "Of course, Uncas, you are too noisy." And he put the offended little beast into his green collecting case.

"I never would have come here," said Mr. Langham, "if it hadn't been for that advertisement."

Arthur frowned slightly.

"You mean——"

"Yes. But I came," said Mr. Langham, "not as a pagan Turk but as a Christian gentleman. I was just about to take passage for Liverpool when I saw your sister Mary looking out at me from *The Four Seasons*. And so I wrote to ask if I could come here. I have lived well, but I am not disappointed. I am very rich——"

"My dear Sam," said Arthur, "you are the best fellow in the world. What do you want of me?"

"To know that you think I'd try my best to make a girl happy if she'd let me."

"A girl?" smiled Arthur. "*Any* girl?"

"In all the world," said Mr. Langham, "there is only one girl."

"If I were you," said Arthur, "I'd ask her what *she* thought about it."

The Seven Darlings

Langham assumed a look of terrible gloom.

"If she didn't think well of it I'd want to cut my throat. I'd rather keep on living in blissful uncertainty, but I wanted *you* to know—*why* I am here, and *why* I want to stay on and on."

"Why, I'm very glad to know," said Arthur, "but surely it's your own affair."

Mr. Langham shook his head.

"Last night," said he, "I was dozing on my little piazza. Who should row by at a distance but Miss Gay and Miss Lee. You know how sounds carry through an Adirondack night? Miss Lee said to Miss Gay: 'I tell you he doesn't. Not *really*. He's just a male flirt.' 'A butter-fly,' said Miss Gay."

"But how do you know they were referring to you?"

"By the way the blessed young things laughed at the word '*butterfly*'. So I wanted you to know that my intentions are tragically serious, no matter what others may say. Whatever I may be, and I have been insulted more than once about my figure and my habits, I am *not* a flirt. I am just as romantic as if I was a living skeleton."

Here Arthur's head went back, and he laughed till the tears came. And Mr. Langham couldn't help laughing, too.

The Seven Darlings

A few moments later he was going over The Inn books with Maud Darling and displaying for her edification an astonishing knowledge of entries and a truly magical facility in figuring. Suddenly, apropos of something not in the least germane, he said:

"Miss Maud, when in your opinion is the most opportune time for a man to propose to a girl?"

"When he's got her alone," said she promptly, "and has just been dazzling her with a display of his erudition and understanding."

And she, whom Mary had described as the one steady sister in the lot, flung him a melting and piercing glance. But Mr. Langham was not deceived.

"I ask you an academic question," he said, "and you give me an absolutely cradle-snatching answer. I may *look* easy, Miss Maud, but there are people who will protect me."

"The best time to propose to a girl? You really want to know? I thought you were just starting one of your jokes."

"If I am," said he, "the joke will be on me. But I *really* want to know."

"The best moment," said she, "is that moment in which she learns that one of her friends or one of her sisters younger than she is engaged to be

The Seven Darlings

married. When an unengaged girl hears of another girl's engagement she has a momentary panic, during which she is helpless and defenseless. That is my best judgment, Mr. Sam Langham. And the older the girl the greater the panic. And now I've betrayed my sex. In fact, I have told you absolutely all that is definitely known about girls."

Just outside the office he met Gay.

"Halloo!" she said.

He only made signs at her and flapped his arms up and down.

"*They* can't talk," he said.

"Who can't talk?"

He held her with a stern glance, and if the word had been hissable, would have hissed it.

"Butterflies," he said.

Then Miss Gay turned the color of a scarlet maple in the fall of the year. Then she squealed and ran.

XVII

"ARE we all here?" asked Mary.
She had summoned her sisters and Arthur
to the office for a conference.

"All except Sam Langham," said Gay.

"I didn't know that he was one of the family,"
said Mary.

"Of course, you *know*," said Gay; "you would.
I was just guessing."

"Well, he isn't," said Mary, trying not to
change color or to enjoy being teased about Mr.
Langham.

The triplets sat in a row upon a bench made
of little birch logs with the bark on. It was not
soft sitting, as Lee whispered, but one had one's
back to the light, and in case one had done something wrong without knowing it and was in for
a scolding, that would prove an immense advantage.

"What I wanted to say," said Mary, "is just
this——"

She stood up and looked rather more at the
triplets than any one else, so that Lee exclaimed,

The Seven Darlings

"Votes for women," and Gay echoed her with, "Yes, but none for poor little girls in their teens."

"Hitherto," continued the orator, "The Inn has been only informally open. It's been more like having a few friends stopping with us. We had to see more or less of them. But after to-day there will be a crowd, and I think it would be more dignified and pleasanter for them if *some* of us kept ourselves a little more to ourselves. What do *you* think, Arthur?"

Arthur looked up sweetly. It was evident that he had not been listening.

"Why, Mary," he said, "I think it might be managed with infinite patience."

The triplets giggled; Maud and Eve exchanged amused looks.

"Arthur," said Mary, "you can make one contribution to this discussion if you want to. You can tell us what you are really thinking about, so that we needn't waste time trying to guess."

"Why," said he gently, "you know I have quite a knack with animals, taming them and training them, and I was wondering if it would be possible to train a snail. *That's* what I was thinking about. I have a couple in my pocket at the moment, and——"

"Never mind *now*," said Mary hurriedly, and

157

she turned to the triplets. "What do *you* think of what I said?"

"I think it was tortuous and involved," said Lee, "and that it would hardly bear repetition."

"It smacked of paternalism," said Gay. And even Phyllis, her mind upon the convalescing Herring, was moved to speak.

"You said it would be more dignified for some of us to keep to ourselves. Perhaps it would. You said it would be pleasanter for the people who are coming here to stay. I doubt it!"

"Bully for you, old girl," shouted Lee and Gay; "sick her!"

Mary moaned. She was proof against their hostilities, but the language in which they were couched pierced her to the marrow.

"I am sure," she said, "that Maud and Eve will agree with me."

"Of course," said Eve.

"Naturally," said Maud.

"There!" exclaimed Mary, with evident triumph.

"We agree," said Eve, "that *some* of us should keep ourselves more to ourselves."

And she looked sternly at the triplets. But then she turned and looked sternly at Mary and rose to her feet.

The Seven Darlings

"We think," she said with a *j'accuse* intonation, "that those who haven't kept themselves to themselves should, and that those who have— shouldn't. Maud and I, for instance, haven't the slightest objection to being fetched for and carried for by attractive young men. Have we, Maud? But hitherto, as must have been obvious to the veriest nincompoop, we have done our own fetching and carrying."

There was a short silence. Mary blushed. Arthur fidgeted. He was wondering if snails preferred the human voice or whistling.

"I'm quite sure," said Maud, "that I haven't been wandering over the hills with future earls, or lost in swamps with interesting invalids, or basked morning after morning in the sunny smile of a gourmet——"

Mary paled under this attack.

"Mr. Langham is altogether different," she said.

"Oh, quite!" cried Lee.

"Utterly, absolutely different!" cried Gay. "To begin with, he's richer; and to end with, he's fatter."

"I shouldn't have said 'fat,'" said Lee. "I should have said 'well-larded,' but then I am something of a stylist."

The Seven Darlings

"Sam Langham," said Mary, "is everybody's friend. And he's an immense help in lots of ways; and then he has a certain definite interest in The Inn. Because, if we need it, he's going to lend us money to carry our accounts."

Gay whispered to Lee behind her hand. Lee giggled.

"What was that?" asked Mary sharply.

"Only a quotation."

"What quotation?"

"Oh, Gay just said something about 'Bought and Paid For.'"

Here Arthur interrupted.

"They're like snails," said he to Mary. "You can only train 'em with infinite patience."

Phyllis rose suddenly and became the cynosure of all eyes except her own, whose particular cynosure at the moment was the floor. She moved toward the door.

"Where are you off to?" asked Mary.

"I'm just going to speak to Chef."

"What about?"

"About some chicken broth."

"For yourself?"

The gentle Phyllis was being goaded beyond endurance. At the door she turned and lifted her great eyes to Mary's.

The Seven Darlings

"No," she said bitterly; "it's for Arthur's snails."

There was a silence.

"If there's any voting," said Phyllis, "I give my proxy to Gay." And she vanished through the door.

"I'm sure," said Mary, "I don't know what the modern young girl is coming to!"

"I know where *that* one is going to," said Gay; "spilling the chicken broth in her unseemly haste."

Then Arthur spoke.

"The modern young girl," he said, "is coming to just where her grandmother came, and by the same road. Girls will be girls. So let's be thankful that the men who have come here so far have been—men. And hopeful that those who are to come will be also. I've lived too much with nature not to know what's natural—when I see it."

"Do you think," said Gay sweetly, "that it's natural for a man to eat as much as Sam Langham does?"

"As natural under the peculiar circumstances," said Arthur, "as it is for you to tease."

Lee rose.

"And you?" said Mary, smiling at last.

161

The Seven Darlings

"Oh," said Lee witheringly, "I have an engagement to carve initials surrounded by a heart on a birch-tree."

And when Lee had gone Gay spoke up.

"I shouldn't wonder," said she, "if, by way of a blind, the baggage had told the truth."

"We should never have called it The Inn," said Mary; "we should have called it The Matrimonial Agency."

"Every pretty girl," said Arthur, "is a matrimonial agency."

At this moment Uncas, the chipmunk, rushed screaming into the room and flung himself into Arthur's lap. Arthur comforted the little beast, and noticed that his nose and face bore fresh evidences of a fight. Uncas complained very bitterly; he was evidently trying to talk.

"Is Stripes hurt?" asked Mary.

"It's his feelings," said Arthur. "He's been made a victim of misplaced confidence. Some young woman has been encouraging him."

"Poor little man!" said Gay with sudden emotion. "Did ums want some nice vasy on ums poor sick nose?"

"He would only lick it off," regretted Arthur.

Mr. Langham's jolly face appeared in the open door.

The Seven Darlings

"I've seen two depart," he said, "and thought maybe the meeting was over."

"It is," said Mary, and, after a moment's hesitation, she boldly joined Mr. Langham and walked off by his side. Even Arthur chuckled.

"And what was the meeting about?" asked Mr. Langham.

"Oh," said Mary, "they won't be serious—not any of them—not even Arthur. So we forgot what the meeting was for, and got into violent discussion about—about natural history."

"And what side did you take?"

"Oh," said Mary, "we were all on the same side—*really*; and that was what made the discussion so violent."

"The day," said Langham, "is young. I feel ripe for an adventure. And you?"

"What sort of an adventure?"

"I thought that if one—or rather if *two* climbed to the top of a very little hill and sat down in the sunshine and admired the view——"

.   .   .   .

Far out on the lake they could see Lee, lolling in the stern of a guide boat. Young Renier was at the oars. But the boat was not being propelled. It was merely drifting.

The Seven Darlings

"I wonder," said Langham, and he watched her face stealthily, "if by any chance those two are really engaged ?"

Was there the least hardening of that lovely, gentle face, the least fleeting expression of that sort of panic which one experiences when arriving at the station in time to see the train pull out but not too late to get aboard by the exercise of swift and energetic manœuvres ?

"Don't say such things !" she said presently. "It's like jumping out from behind a tree and shouting, 'Boo !'"

Mr. Langham smiled complacently and changed the subject. But he said to himself: "That Maud is a clever girl !"

"I suppose," said Mary after a while, "that this is the last really peaceful day we'll have for a long time. To-morrow the place will be full of strange, critical faces. And it will be one long wrestle to make everything go smoothly all the time."

She sighed.

"There are only two ways to success," said Langham. "One is across the wrestling-mat, and one is through the pasture of old Bull Luck. But I'm convinced that The Inn is going to pay very handsomely. There is a fortune in it."

The Seven Darlings

"There mightn't be," said Mary, "if—" and she broke into a peal of embarrassed laughter.

"If what?"

"I was thinking of that *dreadful* picture."

"I often think of it," said Mr. Langham, "and of the first time I saw it."

Mary gave him a somewhat shy look.

"Of course it didn't influence you," she said.

"But it did. And that day I forgot to eat any lunch. I am looking forward," he said, "to warm weather—I enjoy a swim as much as anybody."

"Why is it," said Mary, "that a girl is ashamed when it is her money that attracts a man, and proud when it is her face? Both are equally fortuitous; both are assets in a way—but of the two, it is the money alone which is really useful."

"It sounds convincing to a girl," mused Mr. Langham, "when a man says to her: 'I love you because of your beautiful blue eyes!' But it wouldn't sound in the least convincing if he said: 'I love you because of your beautiful green money!' I don't attempt to explain this. I am merely stating what appears to me to be a fact. But, as you say, money is, or should be, an asset of attraction."

"I suppose beauty is held in greater esteem,"

The Seven Darlings

said Mary, "because it is more democratically bestowed. Money seems to beget hatred because it isn't."

"The French people," said Langham, "hated the nobility because of their wealth and luxury. To-day a common mechanic has more real luxuries at his disposal than poor Louis XVI had, but he hates the rich people who have more than he has—and so it will go on to the end of time."

"Will there always be rich people and poor people?"

"There will always be rich people, but some time they will learn to spend their money more beneficently, and then there won't be any really poor people. If the attic of your house were infected with dirt and vermin you couldn't sleep until it had been cleaned and disinfected. So, some day, rich men will feel about their neighbors; cities about their slums; and nations about other nations. I can imagine a future Uncle Sam saying to a future John Bull"—and he sunk his voice to a comically confidential whisper: " 'Say, old man, I hear you're pressed for ready cash; now't just so happens I'm well fixed at the moment, and—oh, just among friends! Bother the interest!' What a spectacle this world is—it's like the old English schools that Dickens wrote out

The Seven Darlings

of existence—just bullying and hazing all around!
Why, if a country was run on the most elementary
principles of honesty and efficiency, the citizens
of that country would never have occasion to say:
'Our taxes are almost unbearable.' They would
be nudging each other in the streets and saying:
'My, that was a big dividend we got!'"

Mr. Langham only stopped because he was out
of breath. His face was red and shining. He
mopped his brow with his handkerchief.

Mary was almost perfectly happy. She loved
to hear Langham run on and on. His voice was
so pleasant, and his face beamed so with kindness. And from many things which he had from
time to time let slip she was convinced that she
needn't be an old maid unless she wanted to be.
And so to climb a little hill with him, to sit in
the sun, and to admire the view was really an
exciting venture. For she never knew what he
was going to let slip next. And equally exciting
was the fact that if that slip should be in the
nature of a leading question, she could only guess
what her answer would be.

When a man is offered something that he very
much wants—a trifling loan, for instance—his
first instinct is to deny the need. And a girl,
when the man she wants offers himself, usually re-

The Seven Darlings

fuses at the first time of asking. And some, especially rich in girl nature, which is experience of human nature and somewhat short of divine, will persist in refusing even unto the twentieth and thirtieth time.

Mary Darling was in a deep reverie. From this, his eyes twinkling behind their thick glasses, Mr. Langham roused her with the brisk utterance of one of his favorite quotations:

"'General Blank's compliments,'" said he, "'and he reports that the colored troops are turning black in the face.'"

Mary smiled her friendliest smile.

"I was wondering," she said, "what had become of Lee and Renier."

"I have noted," said Mr. Langham, "that she always calls him by his last name, sometimes with the prefix you—'You Renier' put like that. And I was wondering if he ever turns the trick on her."

"Why should he?" asked Mary innocently.

"You have forgotten," said he, "that her last name is Darling." His eyes twinkled with amazing and playful boldness. "You're *all* Darlings," he exclaimed, "and"—a note of self-pity in his voice—"I'm just a fat old stuff!"

"That," said Mary primly, "is perfectly cor-

168

rect, but for three trifling errors—you're not fat, you're not old, and you're not a stuff!"

If she had told him that he was handsome as Apollo he could not have been more pleased.

And so their adventure progressed in the pleasant sunlight that warmed the top of the little hill. No very exciting adventure, you say? And of a shilly-shallying and even snail-like motion?

Oh, you can't be always riding to rescues, and falling over cliffs, and escaping from burning houses.

At that moment, by the purest accident, the tip of Mr. Langham's right forefinger just brushed against Mary's sleeve. And there went through him from head to foot a great thrill, as if trumpets had suddenly sounded.

"I suppose," said Mary, after a little while, "that we ought to be going."

"But I'd rather sit here than eat," said Mr. Langham.

"Honestly? So would I."

"Then," said Mr. Langham, "without exposing ourselves to any other danger than that of starvation, I propose that we lose ourselves—as *other people do*—in short, that we remain here until one or other of us would rather—eat."

The Seven Darlings

"Good gracious," said Mary, "we might be here a week!"

Mr. Langham rose slowly to his feet. Far off he could see pale smoke flitting upward through the tree-tops. He turned and looked into Miss Darling's smiling, upturned face.

"I'll just run down and tell Arthur we're not *really* lost," he said. "But I'll make him promise not to look for us. I'll be right back—almost before you can say 'Jack Robinson.'"

She held out her hands. He took them and helped her to her feet. And then they both laughed aloud.

"Thank Heaven," said Mary, "that whatever else you and I may suffer from, it isn't from insanity—or slim appetites! As a matter of fact, I'm famished."

"Thank God!" said Mr. Langham; "so am I."

And they began to descend the hill. For to keep men and women and adventurers going, the essential thing is food. And there's many a promising romance that has come to nothing for want of a loaf of bread and a jug of wine.

XVIII

IN a certain part of the Land of Cotton, where they grow nothing but rice, Colonel Melville Meredith stood beside the charred foundations of a house and nursed his chin with his hand. With the exception of a sword which the King of Greece had given him, all those possessions which he had considered of value had gone up in smoke with the house of his ancestors. The family portraits were gone, the silver Lamarie, and Lesage, and all the Domingan satinwood. If Colonel Meredith had been an older man, he must almost have wept. But the grip upon his chin was not of one mourning. It was the grip of consideration. He was wondering what sort of a new house he should build upon the foundations of the old.

He must, of course, build upon the old site. There were other good sites among his thousands of acres, but none which was so well planted. A good architect could copy the Taj Mahal for you. But the Pemaque oak is one hundred and seven feet, or less, in circumference, and the avenue of oaks leading from the turnpike, two miles away, was planted in 1653. There were also divers jungles of rhododendrons, laurel, and azalea in the river garden that it had taken no less than a great-grandmother to plant.

"It can't be the first conflagration in the family," he thought. "Everybody's ancestors, at one time or another, must have lost by fire and built again. As for Pemaque—it *was* a lovely old house, but a new house could be just as lovely, and it could have bathrooms and be made rat-proof. And I wouldn't mind if people scratched the floors."

I have said that Colonel Meredith had lost all the possessions which he valued. But of course the land remained, the trees, the duck ponds, the alligator sloughs, and so forth. There remained, also, a robust youth, crowded with experiences and memories of wars and statesmen and of delightful people who live for pleasure. There remained, also—least valuable of all to a man of action and sentiment—a perfectly safe income, derived from bonds, of nearly two hundred and fifty thousand dollars a year. Colonel Meredith was by all odds the richest man in that part of the Land of Cotton, where they grow nothing but rice.

It was piping hot among the foundations of

The Seven Darlings

the old house; the sticky, ticky season had descended upon the Carolina seacoast. The snakes and the lizards were saying among themselves, "Now this is really something like," and were behaving accordingly. Every few minutes a new and ambitious generation of mosquitoes was hatched. The magnolias were going to seed. Colonel Meredith's Gordon setter, a determined expression upon his face, had been scratching himself with almost supercanine speed for the last twenty minutes.

Colonel Meredith scorned ticks, trod with indifference upon snakes, and was not poisoned or even pained by mosquitoes, but he had travelled all over the world and was not averse to being cooler and more comfortable.

"We've got the grandest climate in the world," he thought loyally, "for eight months in the year —but when it comes to summer give me Vera Cruz, Singapore, or even hell. I'll build a home for autumn, winter, and spring, but when it gets to be summer, I'll go away and shoot polar bears."

He whistled his dog and walked thoughtfully to where his automobile was waiting in the shade. His driver, an Irish boy from New York, was in a state of wilt.

"I have determined," said Colonel Meredith,

173

The Seven Darlings

"not to begin building until cool weather. We shall go North to-night. I hope the thought will refresh you. Now we will go back to Mr. Jonstone's. Do you feel able to drive, or shall I ?"

It was typical of the region that the Mr. Jonstone with whom Meredith was stopping should own the best bed of mint south of Washington, and could make the best mint-juleps. The mint-bed was about all he did own. Everything else was heavily mortgaged. Everything, that is, except the family silver and jewels. These Jonstone's grandmother had buried when Sherman came marching through, and had almost immediately forgotten where she had buried them. Jonstone employed one trustworthy negro whose year-around business was to dig for the treasure. There existed a list of the objects buried, which was enough to make even a rich man's palm itch.

"Nothing to-day," said Jonstone as his guest drove up. "And it's about time for a julep."

"I'm going North to-night," said Meredith, "and you're going with me."

They were cousins, second or third, of about the same age. They even looked alike, but whereas Meredith had travelled all over the world, Jonstone had never been south of Savannah or north of Washington.

The Seven Darlings

He began with an ivory toddy-stick to convert sugar and Bourbon into sirup.

"How's that, Mel?" he asked. "And why?"

"Between us two, Bob," said Meredith, "this is one hell of a climate in summer. The brighter we are the quicker we'll get out of it."

"I'd like to go you on that, but aside from the family silver I haven't a penny in the world."

"Bob, I'm sick of offering to lend you money. I'm sick of offering to give you money. There's only one chance left."

Jonstone made a gentle clashing sound with fine ice.

"As you know, my family silver has all gone up in smoke. Now yours hasn't. Suppose you sell me yours. What's it worth?"

"With or without the diamonds?"

"If I should ever marry, it would be advisable to have the diamonds."

"Well," said Jonstone, beginning to turn over a bundle of straws, with the object of selecting four which should be flawless, "I don't want to stick you. We have a complete list of the pieces, with their weights and dates. Some of the New York dealers could tell us what the collection would be worth in the open market. Double that sum in the name of sentiment, and I'll go you."

The Seven Darlings

"I must have a free hand to hunt for the stuff in my own way— It's perfection—you never, never made a better one—now, how about the diamonds?"

"I have the weights. And you know the Jonstones were always particular about water."

"That's why they are all dead but you. Then you'll come?"

Bob Jonstone nodded.

"You'll have to lend me a suit of clothes— but, look here, Mel: suppose the silver and stuff has been lifted—doesn't exist any more? Wouldn't I, in selling it to you, be guilty of sharp practice?"

"Our great - great - grandfather, the Signer, doesn't exist any more, Bob. That silver is somewhere—in some form or other. I pay for it, and it's mine. Does it matter if I never see it or handle it? I shall always be able to allude to it —isn't that enough? As for you, you'll be able to pay all your mortgages, to fix the front door so's it won't have to be kept shut with a keg of nails, and to spend what is necessary on your fields."

"Of course," said Jonstone, who had finished his julep. "It afflicts me to part with what has been in the family so long."

The Seven Darlings

"But you ought to be afflicted."

"Why?"

"Didn't you vote for Wilson?"

Jonstone nodded solemnly.

"Come, then," said Meredith, as if he were pardoning an erring child; "there's just time for one julep and to pack up our things. You'll just love New York. And when we get there we'll make up our minds whether we'll go to Newport or Bar Harbor. Bob, did it ever occur to you that you and I ought to get married? That looks as if it was going to be better than the other, though darker— What's the use of having ancestors if you're not going to be one?"

"Show me a girl as handsome as Sully's portrait of Great-grandmother Pringle, and I'll take notice."

"Why, every other girl in a Broadway chorus has got the old lady skinned to death, Bob!"

"You may be worldly-wiser than me, Mel, but you've lost your reverence. It's always been agreed in the family that Great-grandmother Pringle was the most beautiful woman in the South. And when a man says 'the South,' and refers at the same time to female charms, he has as good as said the whole world."

"Bob, among ourselves, do you really think

The Seven Darlings

Jefferson Davis was a greater man than Abraham
Lincoln?"

"Ssssh!" said Jonstone.

"Do you really think the Southern armies
wiped up the map with the Northern armies
every time they met? And do you really think
that wooden-faced doll that Sully painted has
no equal for beauty north of the Mason and
Dixon line? What you need is travel and experience."

"What's the matter with *you* getting married?
—My God, don't spill that, Mel!"

"There's nothing the matter with it. And
I'll tell you what I'll do: I will if you will."

"They ought to be sisters, seeing as how you
and I have always been like brothers and voted
the Democratic ticket and fought chickens."

"And fed the same ticks and mosquitoes."

"We'll have a double wedding. We'll each be
the other's best man, and they'll each be the
other's best girl."

"No—no; they are each to be our best girls."

"What I mean is——"

"I know what you mean, but you've made this
julep too strong."

"That's *one* thing they can't do in the North."

"What's that?"

The Seven Darlings

"Make a julep."

Meredith considered this at some length. "No, Bob," he said at length, "they can't. But I once met a statesman from Maine who made a thing that looked like a julep, tasted like a julep, and that—I'd say it if it was my dying statement— had the same effect."

"She must be better-looking than Great-grand-mother Pringle," said Jonstone. "She must be able to make a julep, and she must have a sister just like her. Can you lend me a suit of clothes till we get to New York?"

"I can lend you anything from a yachting suit to a Bulgarian uniform."

"And you're sure I'm not imposing on you in the matter of the silver?"

"Sure. I just want to know it's mine."

In the morning, soon after this precious pair had breakfasted, a boy went through the train with newspapers and magazines. He proclaimed in the sweetest Virginian voice that his magazines were just out, but a copy of *The Four Seasons* which Colonel Meredith bought proved not only to be of an ancient date but to have had coffee spilled upon it.

At the moment when this discovery was made, the youthful paper-monger had just swung from

The Seven Darlings

the crawling train to the platform of a way station, so there was no redress. The cousins agreed, laughing, that if a Yankee had played them such a trick they would have wished to cut his heart out, but that, turned upon them by a fellow countryman, it was merely a proof of smartness and push.

"Between you and me, Bob," said Colonel Meredith, "an accurate count of our Southern population would proclaim a villain or two here and there. I was brought up to believe that to be born in a certain region was all that was necessary. But that's not so. I tell you this because I am afraid that when you are meeting people in New York and having a good time you will be wanting to lay down the law, to wit, that one Southerner can whip five Yankees. Don't do it. I will tell you a horrid truth. I was once whipped by a small-sized Frenchman within an inch of my life. He had studied *le boxe* under Carpentier and I hadn't. Did you ever study *le boxe?* No? An Anglo-Saxon imagines that he was born boxing. And it takes a licking by a man of Latin blood to prove to him that he wasn't. Just because people make funny noises and monkey cries when they fight doesn't prove that they are afraid. There is nothing so ridiculous as a baboon going into action and nothing more terrible when he gets there."

"The more you travel, Mel, the more you show a deplorable tendency to foul your own nest."

"*I* run down the South? I like that! But, my dear Bob, there is only one chosen people. And it isn't us." Here he made a significant gesture with his hands, turning the palms up, and they both laughed. "A Jew," he went on, "is what he is because he is a Jew. His good points and his bad are racial. But between two men of our race there is no material resemblance. One is mean, the other generous; one broad, one narrow; one brave, the other not. Do you know why hornless cows give less milk than horned cows? Because there are fewer of them. Do you know why there are more honest men in the North, and pretty girls, than there are in the South? Simply because there are more men and more girls. It also follows that there are more dishonest men and ugly girls; more of everything, in fact."

He was slowly turning over the pages of *The Four Seasons*, looking always, with Pemaque in mind, at pictures of country houses. Suddenly he closed the magazine, looked pensively out of the window, and began to whistle with piercing sweetness. He once moie opened the magazine, but this time with great caution as if he was half afraid that something disagreeable would jump out at him. Nothing did, however. He folded the magazine back upon itself and held it close to his eyes, then far off, then at mid-distance.

"What's the matter with you?" said Bob Jonstone.

"Nothing," said Meredith, "only I'm thinking there ought to be six of us instead of only two. Look at that page and tell me where we're going to spend the summer."

Jonstone took the magazine and saw the six Darling sisters sitting on the float in their bathing-dresses. Presently he smiled and said: "You've just won an argument, Mel."

"How's that?"

"Why, in the South there wouldn't be so many of them—but maybe they are not always there. Maybe they were only there last summer."

"Well, we can find out where they've gone, can't we?"

"It doesn't seem in strict good breeding to pursue ladies one doesn't know."

"Why, bless you, I chased all over Europe

The Seven Darlings

after a face I saw in *The Sketch*, only to find out that she was willing to marry anybody with money and had a voice like a guinea-hen. And after I'd found that out, she chased *me* all over Europe and as far East as Cairo."

"I've never been chased by a woman," said Jonstone a little wistfully. "What happened in the end?"

"I left Cairo between two days, fled away into the desert with some people just stepped out of the Bible, and never came back."

"Suppose she hadn't been willing to marry you and had had a voice like a dove?"

"Don't suppose. We are on a new quest."

"What is the Adirondacks?"

"We wouldn't think much of it in the South. It's a place where you are always cool and clean and can drink the nearest water. The trout don't eat mud and haven't got long white whiskers, and the deer are bigger than dogs, and you don't go to sleep at night. The night just comes and puts you to sleep. It's just like Bar Harbor—only a little more so in some ways and a little less so in others."

Jonstone spread *The Four Seasons* wide open upon his knees.

"Let's agree right now," he said, "which each

of us thinks is the prettiest. It would be dreadful after travelling so far if we were both to pick on the same one."

"We would have to fight a duel," said Meredith, "with swords, and considering that you could never even sharpen a pencil without cutting yourself——"

"A boy wouldn't come along," said Jonstone, "and sell us a copy of a magazine months old if fate hadn't meant us to see this picture. I think I like the third one from the end."

"I think I like the three that look just alike."

"That is because you have travelled in Turkey. You never seem to remember that you are a Christian gentleman."

XIX

WHEN they found out how much the buried silver was worth—the inventory was very thorough in the matter of description, dates, and weights—Mr. Bob Jonstone burst out laughing. But Colonel Meredith, although determined to stand by his bargain whatever the cash cost, looked like a man who has just missed the last train.

"I haven't got that much money loose, Bob," he said, "but I can raise it in a few days and then we'll execute a bill of sale. Meanwhile, allow me to congratulate you on your accession to the aristocracy."

"Aristocracy? It's blood that counts—not money."

"According to the old democracy, yes. According to the new, distinguished people pay an income tax and common people don't. And you, a moment ago, before the valuation was completed, were a very common fellow, indeed."

"Mel, I had no idea that old junk was worth so much."

The Seven Darlings

"You hadn't? Well, it's worth more. I'm getting a bargain. Thank the Lord you're a gentleman, so there's no danger of your backing out."

Jonstone seized his cousin's hand and pressed it affectionately.

"Mel," he said, "can you afford to do this thing? God knows the money will make all the difference in the world to me! But in taking it I don't feel any too noble."

"It was always ridiculous for me to be rich and for you to be poor. That's done with. I'm still rich, thank God!—and you're well-to-do. You can travel if you like, breed horses, install plumbing, burn coal, and marry."

"If I was sure that the silver would ever be turned up, I wouldn't feel so sheepish."

"As long as you don't look sheepish or act sheepish—suppose that now, after a slight fortification, we visit a tailor. It is necessary for you to dress according to your station in life."

Their first day in New York was immensely amusing to both of them. Meredith was coming back to it after a long absence; Jonstone was seeing it for the first time, and for the first time his pockets were full of money that he did not owe. Now, New York is one of the finest summer re-

sorts in the world. Do not pity the poor business
man who sends his family to the mountains for
the hot weather, for while they are burned by
the sun and fed an interminable succession of
blueberry pies, he basks in the cool of electric
fans and dines on the fat of the land. His business may worry him, but there is no earthly
use in his attending to it. That is done for him.
He can skip away when he pleases for an afternoon's golf or tennis. Somebody's motor is always going somewhere where there is pleasure to
be found and laughter. The lights of Luna Park
are brighter than the Bar Harbor stars, and the
ocean which pounds upon Long Beach is just as
salt as that which thunders against Great Head—
and about twice as warm. For pure torture give
me a swim anywhere north of Cape Cod. Merely
to step into such water is like having one's foot
bitten off by a shark.

It did not take Jonstone long to acknowledge
that New York is even bigger than Richmond,
Virginia, and even livelier. The discovery of a
superannuated mosquito in his bathroom had
made him feel at home, and the fact that the head
bartender in the hotel, though a native of Ire-
land, fashioned a delicious julep.

But his equanimity came very near to being

upset in the subway. He felt a hand slipping into his pocket and caught it by the wrist. He had a grip like looped wire twisted with pinchers. The would-be thief uttered a startled shriek and was presently turned over to a policeman.

All the way to the station-house Mr. Jonstone talked excitedly and triumphantly to his cousin.

"Yes, sir," he said, "you had me groggy with your high buildings and your Aladdin-cave stores and your taxicabs and park systems. But by the Everlasting, sir, this would never have happened to me south of the Mason and Dixon line. No, sir; we may be short on show but we're long on honesty down there. I don't even have to lock my door at night."

"That's because the lock's broken and you've always kept it shut with a keg of nails. There are more pickpockets in New York than in Charleston, but only because there are more pockets to pick."

"I don't get you," said Jonstone stiffly. A little later he did.

The culprit was asked his name by a formidable desk sergeant.

"Stephen Breckenridge."

Bob Jonstone gasped.

"Where do you come from?"

The Seven Darlings

"Lexington, Kentucky."

Colonel Meredith let forth a howl of laughter. And after he had been frowned into decorum by the sergeant, he continued for a long time to look as if he was going to burst.

For some hours Mr. Jonstone was moody and unamused. Then suddenly he broke into a winning smile.

"Mel," he said, "I wouldn't have minded so much if he had been smart enough to get my money. It was bad finding out that he was a compatriot of ours, but much more to realize that he was a fool."

XX

MR. LANGHAM was consulted about everything. And it was to him that Maud
Darling took Meredith's letter asking for accommodations.

"We've only two rooms left," she said, "and
such nice people have come, or are coming, that
it would be an awful pity if we had the bad luck
to fill up with two men that weren't nice. Did
you ever hear of a Colonel Meredith?"

"Is that his letter? May I look?"

Mr. Langham read the letter through very
carefully. Then he said, looking at her over the
tops of his thick glasses:

"I don't know if you know it, but I have made
quite a study of handwritings. The writer of
this letter is a gentleman—a Southern gentleman,
if I am not mistaken. Accepting this premise,
we may assume that his friend Mr. Robert Middleton Jonstone is also a Southern gentleman.
Middleton, in fact, is pure South Carolinian."

"But if they are from South Carolina, wouldn't

our terms stagger them? I've always understood that Southern gentlemen lost all their money in the war."

"Nevertheless," said Mr. Langham, "this is the writing of a rich man."

"How *can* you know that?"

"I tell you that I have made a study of handwriting. It is also the writing of a horse-loving, war-loving, much-travelled man—in the late twenties."

"You will tell me next that he is about five feet ten inches tall, has blue eyes, and is handsome as an angel."

"You take the words out of my mouth, Miss Maud."

"Tell me more." She was laughing now.

"He is very handsome, but not as angels are —his eyes are too bold and roving. If he wasn't a good man he would be a very bad man. There was a time, even, when strong drink appealed to him. He is quixotically brave and generous. And I should by all means advise you to let him have his accommodations."

"I can never tell when you are joking."

"I was never more serious in my life. Shall I tell you something else that I have deduced?"

"Please."

The Seven Darlings

"Well, then, he isn't married, Miss Maud, and he is a great catch!"

Miss Maud blushed a trifle.

"I don't know if you know it," she said, "but I have made a profound study of palmistry. Will you lend me your hand a moment?"

"Very willingly. And I don't care if some one were to see us."

She studied his palm with great sternness.

"I read here," she said, "with regret, that you are an outrageous flirt. It seems also that you are something of a fraud."

"One more calumny," exclaimed Mr. Langham, "and I withdraw my hand with a gesture of supreme indignation."

But she held him very tightly by the fingers.

"And this little line," she cried, "tells me that you have known Colonel Meredith intimately for years and that you never studied handwriting in all your born days."

Mr. Langham began to chuckle all over.

"The next time," he said, "that people tell me you are easily imposed on, I shall deny it."

"You *do* know him?"

He blinked and nodded like a wise owl.

"Shall I write or telegraph?"

"You will use your own judgment."

"I read here," she said, "with regret, that you are an
outrageous flirt"

The Seven Darlings

So she did both. She wrote out a telegram and sent it to Carrytown in the *Streak*. And she tried to picture in her mind a young man who should look like an angel if his eyes weren't too bold and roving.

Her sisters and her brother all proclaimed that Maud was a really sensible person. But none of them knew how really sensible she was.

She was, for instance, more interested in Colonel Meredith than in his cousin Mr. Jonstone, and for the simple reason that she knew the one to be rich and handsome and knew nothing whatever about the other.

XXI

M R. LANGHAM was at the float to welcome
the two Carolinians.

"You have," he complimented Colonel Meredith, "once more proved the ability to land on
your feet in a soft spot. You will be more comfortable here, better fed, better laundered than
anywhere else in the world."

As they strolled from the float to the office,
Mr. Jonstone looked about him a little uneasily.
Not one of the beautiful girls who had looked
into his eyes from the page of *The Four Seasons*
was in sight, or, indeed, any girl, woman, or female
of any sort whatever. He had led himself to
expect a resort crowded with rustling and starchy
boarders. He found himself, instead, in a primeval pine forest in which were sheltered many
low, austere buildings of logs, above whose great
chimneys stood vertical columns of pale smoke.
It was not yet dusk, but the air among the long
shadows had an icy quality and was heavily
charged with the odor of balsam. It was difficult
to believe the season summer, and Mr. Jonstone

The Seven Darlings

was reminded of December evenings in the Carolinas.

"This is the office," said Mr. Langham, and he ushered them into the presence of a bright birch fire and Maud Darling. Each of the Carolinians drew a quick breath and bowed as if before royalty. Mr. Langham presented them to Miss Darling. She begged them to write their names in the guest book and to warm themselves at the fire.

"And then," said Sam Langham, "I'll shake them up a cocktail and show them their house."

"Are we to have a whole house to ourselves?" asked Colonel Meredith. He had not yet taken his eyes from Maud Darling's face.

"It's only two rooms: bath, parlor, and piazza," she explained.

"That last?" asked Mr. Jonstone.

"It's the same thing as a 'poach,'" explained Mr. Langham with a sly twinkle in his eyes.

"It's to sit on and enjoy the view from," added Maud.

"But I don't want to admire the view," complained Colonel Meredith. "I want to lounge about the office. It's the prerogative of every American citizen to lounge about the office of his hotel."

The Seven Darlings

Colonel Meredith had yet to take his eyes from Maud Darling's face. And it was with protest written all over it that he at length followed his cousin and Mr. Langham into the open air.

The three were presently sampling a cocktail of the latter's shaking in the latter's snug little house, and speech was loosened in their mouths.

"Darling, *père*," explained Sam Langham, "went broke. He used to run this place as it is run now, with this difference: that in the old days he put up the money, while now it is the guests who pay. Two years ago the Miss Darling you just met was one of the greatest heiresses in America; now she keeps books and makes out bills."

"And are there truly five others equally lovely?" asked Colonel Meredith.

"Some people think that the oldest of the six is also the loveliest," said Sam Langham, loyal to the choice of his own heart. "But they are all very lovely."

To the Carolinians, warmed by Langham's cocktail, it seemed pitiful that six beautiful girls who had had so much should now have so little. And with a little encouragement they would have been moved to the expression of exaggerated

The Seven Darlings

sentiments. It was Maud, however, and not the others, who had aroused these feelings in their breasts. The desire to benefit her by some secret action—and then to be found out—was very strong in them both.

Langham left them after a time and they began to dress for dinner. Usually they had a great deal to say to each other; often they disputed and were gorgeously insolent to each other about the most trifling things, but on the present occasion their one desire was to dress as rapidly as possible and to visit the office upon some pretext or other.

When Colonel Meredith from the engulfment of a starched shirt announced that he had several letters to write and wondered where one could buy postage-stamps, it afforded Bob Jonstone malicious satisfaction to inform him that the "little drawer in their writing-table contained not only plenty of twos but fives and a strip of special deliveries."

"All I have to think about," said he, "is my laundry. I suppose they can tell me at the office."

"*They?*" exclaimed Colonel Meredith.

As he spoke the collar button sprang like a slippery cherry-stone from between his thumb

The Seven Darlings

and forefinger, fell in the exact middle of the room in a perfectly bare place, and disappeared. Up to this moment the cousins had remained on even terms in the race to be dressed first. But now Mr. Jonstone gained and, before the collar button was found, had given a parting "slick" to his hair and gone out.

It was now dark, and the woodland streets of The Camp were lighted by lanterns. Windows were bright-yellow rectangles. A wind had risen and the lake could be heard slapping against the rocky shore.

Maud Darling had left the office long enough to change from tailor-made tweeds to the simplest white muslin. She was adding up a column in a fat book. She looked golden in the firelight and the lamplight, and resembled some heavenly being but for the fact that, for the moment, she was puzzled to discover the sum of seven and five and was biting the end of her pencil. The divine muse of Inspiration lives in the "other" ends of pens and pencils. The world owes many of its masterpieces of literature and invention to reflective nibbling at these instruments, and if I were a teacher I should think twice before I told my pupils to take their pencils out of their mouths.

The Seven Darlings

Mr. Jonstone knocked on the open door of the office.

"This is the office," said Miss Maud Darling; "you don't have to knock. Is anything not right?"

"Everything is absolutely perfect," bowed Mr. Jonstone. "But you are busy. I could come again. I only wanted to ask about sending some things to a laundry."

"You're not supposed to think about that," said Maud. "There is a clothes-bag in the big closet in your bedroom and my sister Eve does the rest."

"Oh, but I couldn't allow——"

"Not with her own hands, of course; she merely oversees the laundry and keeps it up to the mark. But if you like your things to be done in any special way you must see her and explain."

"In my home," said Jonstone, "my old mammy does all the washing and most everything else, and I wouldn't dare to find fault. She would follow me up-stairs and down scolding all the time if I did. You see, though she isn't a slave any more, she's never had any wages, and so she takes it out in privileges and prerogatives."

"No wages ever since the Civil War!" exclaimed Maud.

The Seven Darlings

"We had to have servants," he explained, "and until the other day there was never any money to pay them with. We had nothing but the plantation and the family silver."

"And of course you couldn't part with that. In the North when we get hard up we sell anything we've got. But in the South you don't, and I've always admired that trait in you beyond measure."

"In that case," said Mr. Jonstone, turning a little pale, "it is my duty to tell you that the other day I parted with my silver in exchange for a large sum of money. I made up my mind that I had only one life to live and that I was sick of being poor."

Maud smiled.

"If you want to keep your ill-gotten gains," she said, "you ought never to have come to this place. Wasn't there some kind friend to tell you that our prices are absolutely prohibitive? We haven't gone into business for fun but with the intention of making money hand over fist. It's only fair to warn you."

She imagined that, at the outside, he might have received a couple of thousand dollars for his family silver, and it seemed wicked that he should be allowed to part with this little capital for food, lodging, and a little trout-fishing.

The Seven Darlings

"My silver," he said, "turned out to be worth a lot of money, and I have put it all in trust for myself, so that my wife and children shall never want."

A flicker of disappointment appeared in Maud Darling's eyes.

"But I didn't know you were married," she said lamely.

"Oh, I'm not—yet!" he exclaimed joyfully. "But I mean to be."

"Engaged?" she asked.

"Hope to be—mean to be," he confessed.

And at this moment Colonel Melville Meredith came in out of the night. Having bowed very low to Miss Darling, he turned to his cousin.

"Did Langham find you?" he asked.

"No."

"Well, he's a-waiting at our house. I said I thought you'd be right back."

"Then we—" began Jonstone.

"Not we—*you*," said his cousin, malice in his eyes. "I want to ask Miss Darling some questions about telegrams and special messages by telephone."

Bob Jonstone withdrew himself with the utmost reluctance.

"We have a telephone that connects us with

the telegraph office at Carrytown," Maud began, but Colonel Meredith interrupted almost rudely.

"We engaged our rooms for ten days only," he said, "but I want to keep them for the rest of the summer. Please don't tell me that they are promised to some one else."

"But they are," said she; "I'm very sorry."

"Can't you possibly keep us?"

She shook her fine head less in negation than reflection.

"I don't see how," she said finally, "unless some one gives out at the last minute. There are just so many rooms and just so many applicants."

"How long," he asked, "would it take to build a little house for my cousin and me?"

"If we got all the carpenters from Carrytown," said Maud, "it could be done very quickly. But——"

"Now you are going to make some other objection!"

"I was only going to say that if you wanted to go camping for a few weeks, we could supply you with everything needful. We have first-rate tents for just that sort of thing."

"But we don't want to go camping. We want to stay here."

"Exactly. There is no reason why you

shouldn't pitch your tent in the main street of this camp and live in it."

"That's just what we'll do," said Colonel Meredith, "and to-morrow we'll pick out the site for the tent—if you'll help us."

XXII

EARLY the next morning Colonel Meredith and his cousin Bob Jonstone presented themselves at the office dressed for walking. Butter would not have melted in their mouths.

"Can you come now and help us pick out a site for the tent?" asked the youthful colonel.

Maud was rather busy that morning, but she closed her ledger, selected a walking-stick, and smiled her willingness to aid them.

"It will seem more like real camping-out," said Mr. Jonstone, "if we don't pitch our tent right in the midst of things. Suppose we take a boat and row along the shores of the lake, keeping our eyes peeled."

Maud was not averse to going for a row with two handsome and agreeable young men. They selected a guide boat and insisted on helping her in and cautioning her about sitting in the middle. Maud had almost literally been brought up in a guide boat, but she only smiled discreetly. The cousins matched for places. As Maud sat in the stern with a paddle for steering, Colonel Meredith, who won the toss, elected to row stroke. Bob Jonstone climbed with gingerness and melancholy into the bow. Not only was he a long way from that beautiful girl, but Meredith's head and shoulders almost completely blanketed his view of her.

"We ought to row English style," he said.

"What is English style, and why ought we to row that way?"

"In the American shells," explained Jonstone, "the men sit in the middle. In the English shells each man sits as far from his rowlock as possible."

"Why?" asked Meredith, who understood his cousin's predicament perfectly.

"So's to get more leverage," explained Jonstone darkly.

"It's for Miss Darling to say," said Meredith. "Which style do you prefer, Miss Darling, English or American?"

"I think the American will be more comfortable for you both and safer for us all," said she.

"There!" exclaimed the man of war, "what did I tell you?"

"But—" continued Maud.

"I could have told you there would be a 'but,'" interrupted Jonstone triumphantly.

The Seven Darlings

"But," repeated Maud, "I'm coxswain, and I want to see what every man in my boat is doing."

So they rowed English style.

"It's like a dinner-party," explained Maud to Colonel Meredith, who appeared slightly discomforted. "Don't you know how annoying it is when there's a tall centrepiece and you can't see who's across the table from you?"

"Even if you don't want to look at him when you have found out who he is," agreed Meredith. "Exactly."

They came to a bold headland of granite crowned with a half-dozen old pines that leaned waterward.

"That's rather a wonderful site, I think," said Maud.

"Where?" said the gentlemen, turning to look over their shoulders. Then, "It looks well enough from the water," said Jonstone, "but we ought not to choose wildly."

"Let us land," said Colonel Meredith, "and explore."

They landed and began at once to find reasons for pitching the tent on the promontory and reasons for not pitching it.

"The site is open and airy," said Jonstone.

"It is," said Colonel Meredith. "But, in case of

a southwest gale, our tent would be blown inside out."

A moment later, "How about drinking-water?" asked the experienced military man.

"I regret to say that I have just stepped into a likely spring," said Jonstone.

"We must sit down and wait till it clears."

When the spring once more bubbled clean and undefiled Mr. Jonstone scooped up two palmfuls of water and drank.

"Delicious!" he cried.

Colonel Meredith then sampled the spring and shook his head darkly.

"This spring has a main attribute of drinking-water," he said; "it is wet. Otherwise——"

"What's the matter with my spring?" demanded his cousin.

"Silica, my dear fellow—silica. And you know very well that silica to a man of your inherited tendencies spells gout."

Jonstone nodded gravely.

"I'm afraid that settles it." And he turned to Maud Darling. "I can keep clear of gout," he explained, "only just as long as I keep my system free from silica."

"Do you usually manage to?" asked Maud, very much puzzled.

The Seven Darlings

"So far," he said, "I have *always* managed to."

"Then you have never suffered from gout?"

"Never. But now, having drunk at this spring, I have reason to fear the worst. It will take at least a week to get that one drink out of my system."

And so they passed from the promontory with the pine-trees to a little cove with a sandy beach, from this to a wooded island not much bigger than a tennis-court. In every suggested site Jonstone found multitudinous charms and advantages, while Colonel Meredith, from the depths of his military experience, produced objections of the first water. For to be as long as possible in the company of that beautiful girl was the end which both sought.

Maud had gone upon the expedition in good faith, but when its true object dawned upon her she was not in the least displeased. The very obvious worship which the Carolinians had for her beauty was not so personal as to make her uncomfortable. It was rather the worship of two artists for art itself than for a particular masterpiece. Of the six beautiful Darlings Maud had had the least experience of young men. She was given to fits of shyness which passed with some as reserve, with others as a kind of common-

"Do you usually manage to?" asked Maud, very much puzzled

The Seven Darlings

sense and matter-of-fact way of looking at life. The triplets, young as they were, surpassed the other three in conquests and experience. And this was not because they were more lovely and more charming but because they had been a little spoiled by their father and brought into the limelight before their time. Furthermore, with the exception of Phyllis, perhaps, they were maidens of action to whom there was no recourse in books or reflection. Such accomplishments as drawing and music had not been forced upon them. They could not have made a living teaching school. But Lee and Gay certainly could have taught the young idea how to shoot, how to throw a fly, and how to come in out of the wet when no house was handy. As for Phyllis, she would have been as like them as one pea is like two others but for the fact that at the age of two she had succeeded in letting off a 45-90 rifle which some fool had left about loaded and had thereby frightened her early sporting promises to death. But it was only of weapons, squirming fish, boats, and thunder storms that she was shy. Young gentlemen had no terrors for her, and she preferred the stupidest of these to the cleverest of books.

Mary, Maud, and Eve had wasted a great part of their young lives upon education. They could play the piano pretty well (you couldn't tell which was playing); they sang charmingly; they knew French and German; they could spell English, and even speak it correctly, a power which they had sometimes found occasion to exercise when in the company of foreign diplomatists. The change in their case from girlhood to young womanhood had been sudden and prearranged: in each case a tremendous ball upon a given date. The triplets had never "come out."

If Lee or Gay had been the victim of the present conspiracy, the gentlemen from Carolina would have found their hands full and overflowing. They would have been teased and misconstrued within an inch of their lives; but Maud Darling was genuinely moved by the candor and chivalry of their combined attentions. There was a genuine joyousness in her heart, and she did not care whether they got her home in time for lunch or not. And it was only a strong sense of duty which caused her to point out the high position attained by the sun in the heavens.

With reluctance the trio gave up the hopeless search for a camp site and started for home upon a long diagonal across the lake. It was just then, as if a signal had been given, that the whole surface of the lake became ruffled as when a piece of

The Seven Darlings

blue velvet is rubbed the wrong way, and a strong wind began to blow in Maud's face and upon the backs of the rowers.

Several hours of steady rowing had had its effect upon unaccustomed hands. It was now necessary to pull strongly, and blisters grew swiftly from small beginnings and burst in the palms of the Carolinians. Maud came to their rescue with her steering paddle, but the wind, bent upon having sport with them, sounded a higher note, and the guide boat no longer seemed quick to the least propulsion and light on the water, but as if blunt forward, high to the winds, and half full of stones. She did not run between strokes but came to dead stops, and sometimes, during strong gusts, actually appeared to lose ground.

The surface of the lake didn't as yet testify truly to the full strength of the wind. But soon the little waves grew taller, the intervals between them wider, and their crests began to be blown from them in white spray. The heavens darkened more and more, and to the northeast the sky-line was gradually blotted out as if by soft gray smoke.

"We're going to have rain," said Maud, "and we're going to have fog. So we'd better hurry a little."

The Seven Darlings

"Hurry?" thought the Carolinians sadly. And they redoubled their efforts, with the result that they began to catch crabs.

"Some one ought to see us and send a launch," said Maud.

At that moment, as the wind flattens a field of wheat to the ground, the waves bent and lay down before a veritable blast of black rain. It would have taken more than human strength to hold the guide boat to her course. Maud paddled desperately for a quarter of a minute and gave up. The boat swung sharply on her keel, rocked dangerously, and, once more light and sentient, a creature of life, made off bounding before the gale.

"We are very sorry," said the Carolinians, "but the skin is all off our hands, and at the best we are indifferent boatmen."

"The point is this," said Maud: "Can you swim?"

"I can," said Colonel Meredith, "but I am extremely sorry to confess that my cousin's aquatic education has been neglected. Where he lives every pool contains crocodiles, leeches, snapping-turtles, and water-moccasins, and the incentive to bathing for pleasure is slight."

"Don't worry about me," said Mr. Jonstone. "I can cling to the boat until the millennium."

The Seven Darlings

"We shan't upset—probably," said Maud. "It will be better if you two sit in the bottom of the boat. I'll try to steer and hold her steady. This isn't the first time I've been blown off shore and then on shore. I suppose I ought to apologize for the weather, but it really isn't my fault. Who would have thought this morning that we were in for a storm?"

"If only you don't mind," said Colonel Meredith. "It's all *our* fault. You probably didn't want to come. You just came to be friendly and kind, and now you are hungry and wet to the skin——"

"But," interrupted Bob Jonstone, "if only you will forget all that and think what pleasure we are having."

"I can't hear what you say," called Maud.

"I beg your pardon," shouted Mr. Jonstone. "I didn't quite catch that. What did Miss Darling say, Mel?"

"She said she wanted to talk to me and for you to shut up."

Mr. Jonstone made a playful but powerful swing at his cousin, and the guide boat, as if suddenly tired of her passengers, calmly upset and spilled them out.

A moment later the true gallantry of Mr. Bob

The Seven Darlings

Jonstone showed forth in glorious colors. Having risen to the surface and made good his hold upon the overturned boat, he proposed very humbly, as amends for causing the accident, to let go and drown.

"If you do," said Maud, excitement overcoming her sense of the ridiculous, "I'll never speak to you again."

Colonel Meredith opened his mouth to laugh and closed it a little hastily on about a pint of water.

XXIII

THE water was so rough, the weather so thick, and their point of view so very low down in the world that Maud and the Carolinians could neither see the shore from which they had departed nor that toward which they were slowly drifting. The surface water was warm, however, owing to a week of sunshine, and it was not necessary to drop one's legs into the icy stratum beneath.

It is curious that what the three complained of the most was the incessant, leaden rain. Their faces were colder than their bodies. They admitted that they had never been so wet in all their lives. Maud and Colonel Meredith, not content with the slow drifting, kicked vigorously; but Bob Jonstone had all he could do to cling to the guide boat and keep his head above water. His legs had a way of suddenly rising toward the surface and wrapping themselves half around the submerged boat. An effort was made to right the boat and bale her out. But Maud's water-soaked skirt and a sudden case of rattles on the part of Jonstone prevented the success of the manœuvre.

Half an hour passed.

"Personally," said Jonstone, "I've had about enough of this."

His clinging hands looked white and thin; the knuckles were beginning to turn blue. He had a drawn expression about the mouth, but his eyes were bright and resolute.

"I've always understood," said Colonel Meredith, "that girls suffer less than men from total submersion in cold water. I sincerely hope, Miss Darling, that this is so."

"Oh, I'm not suffering," said she; "not yet. My father used to let us go in sometimes when there was a skin of ice along shore. So please don't worry about me."

Mr. Jonstone's teeth began to chatter very steadily and loudly. And just then Maud raised herself a little, craned her neck, and had a glimpse of the shore—a long, half-submerged point, almost but not quite obliterated by the fog and the splashing rain.

"Land ho!" said she joyfully. "All's well. There's a big shallow off here; we'll be able to wade in a minute."

And, indeed, in less than a minute Bob Jon-

stone's feet found the hard sand bottom. And
in a very short time three shipwrecked mariners
had waded ashore and dragged the guide boat
into a clump of bushes.

"And now what?" asked Colonel Meredith.

"And now," said Maud, "the luck has changed.
Half a mile from here is a cave where we used to
have picnics. There's an axe there, matches, and
probably a tin of cigarettes, and possibly things
to eat. It's all up-hill from here, and if you two
follow me and keep up, you'll be warm before we
get there."

Her wet clothes clung to her, and she went
before them like some swift woodland goddess.
Their spirits rose, and with them their voices, so
that the deer and other animals of the neighbor-
ing woods were disturbed and annoyed in the
shelters which they had chosen from the rain.
Sometimes Maud ran; sometimes she merely
moved swiftly; but now and then while the way
was still among the dense waterside alders, she
broke her way through with fine strength, reck-
less of scratches.

The following Carolinians began to worship the
ground she trod and to stumble heavily upon it.
They were not used to walking. It had always
been their custom to go from place to place upon

horses. They panted aloud. They began to suspect themselves of heart trouble, and they had one heavy fall apiece.

Suddenly Maud came to a dead stop.

"I smell smoke," she said. "Some one is here before us. That's good luck, too."

She felt her way along the face of a great bowlder and was seen to enter the narrow mouth of a cave.

"Who's here?" she called cheerfully.

The passageway into the cave twisted like the letter S so that you came suddenly upon the main cavity. This—a space as large as a ball-room—had a smooth floor of sand, broken by one or two ridges of granite. At the farther end burned a bright fire, most of whose smoke after slow, aimless drifting was strongly sucked upward through a hole in the roof. Closely gathered about this fire were four men, who looked like rather dissolute specimens of the Adirondack guide, and a young woman with an old face. Maud's quick eyes noted two rusty Winchester rifles, a leather mail-bag, and the depressing fact that the men had not shaved for many days.

It is always awkward to enter your own private cave and find it occupied by strangers.

"You mustn't mind," said Maud, smiling upon

"And now what?" asked Colonel Meredith

them, "if we share the fire. It's really our cave
and our firewood."

"Sorry, miss," said one of the men gruffly,
"but when it comes on to rain like this a man
makes bold of any shelter that offers."

"Of course," said Maud. "I'm glad you did.
We'll just dry ourselves and go."

She seated herself with a Carolinian on either
side, and their clothes began to send up clouds
of steam.

The young woman with the old face, having
devoured Maud with hungry, sad eyes, spoke in
a shy, colorless voice.

"It would be better, miss, if you was to let
the boys go outside. I could lend you my blanket
while your clothes dried."

"That's very good of you," said Maud, "but
I'm very warm and comfortable and drying out
nicely."

One of the men rose, grinned awkwardly, and
said:

"I'll just have a look at the weather." With
affected carelessness he caught up one of the Winchesters and passed from sight toward the en-
trance of the cave. This manœuvre seemed to
have a cheering effect upon the other three.

"What do you find to shoot at this time of

year?" asked Maud, and she smiled with great innocence.

"The game-laws," said the man who had spoken first, "weren't written for poor men."

"Don't tell me," exclaimed Maud, "that you've got a couple of partridges or even venison just waiting to be cooked and eaten!"

"No such luck," said the man.

Neither of the Carolinians had spoken. They steamed pleasantly and appeared to be looking for pictures in the hot embers. Their eyes seemed to have sunk deeper into their skulls. Men who were familiar with them would have known that they were very angry about something and as dangerous as a couple of rattlesnakes. After a long while they exchanged a few words in low voices and a strange tongue. It was the dialect of the Sea Island negroes—the purest African grafted on English so pure that nobody speaks it nowadays.

"What say?" asked one of the strangers roughly.

Colonel Meredith turned his eyes slowly upon the speaker.

"I remarked to my cousin," said he icily, "that in our part of the world even the lowest convict knows enough to rise to his feet when a lady enters the room and to apologize for being alive."

"In the North Woods," said the man sulkily, "no one stands on ceremony. If you don't like our manners, Mr. Baltimore Oriole, you can lump 'em, see?"

"I see," said Colonel Meredith quietly, "that that leather mail-bag over there belongs to the United States Government. And I have a strong suspicion, my man, that you and your allies were concerned in the late hold-up perpetrated on the Montreal express. And I shall certainly make it my business to report you as suspicious characters to the proper authorities."

"That'll be too easy," said the man. "And suppose we was what you think, what would we be doing in the meantime? I ask you *what?*"

Mr. Jonstone interrupted in a soft voice.

"Oh, quit blustering and threatening," he said.

"Say," said a man who had not yet spoken, "do you two sprigs of jasmine ever patronize the 'movies'? And, if so, did you ever look your fill on a film called 'Held for Ransom'? You folks has a look of being kind o' well to do, and it looks to me as if you'd have to pay for it."

"Why quarrel with them?" said Maud, with gravity and displeasure in her voice, but no fear.

The Seven Darlings

"Things are bad enough as they are. I saw that the minute we came in. Just one minute too late, it seems."

"That's horse-sense," admitted one of the men. "And when this rain holds up, one of us will take a message to your folks saying as how you are stopping at an expensive hotel and haven't got money enough to pay your bill."

"And that," said Colonel Meredith, "will only leave three of you to guard us. Once," he turned to Maud, "I spent six hours in a Turkish prison."

"What happened?" she asked.

"I didn't like it," he said, "and left."

"This ain't Turkey, young feller, and we ain't Turks. If you don't like the cave you can lump it, but you can't leave."

"We don't intend to leave till it stops raining," put in Mr. Jonstone sweetly.

"Miss Darling," said Colonel Meredith, "you don't feel chilled, do you? You mustn't take this adventure seriously. These people are desperate characters, but they haven't the mental force to be dangerous. It will be the greatest pleasure in the world both to my cousin and myself to see that no harm befalls you." He turned once more to the unshaven men about the fire.

"Have you got anything worth while in that

222

mail-bag?" he asked. "I read that the safe in the Montreal express only contained a few hundred dollars. Hardly worth risking prison for—was it?"

"We'll have enough to risk prison for before we get through with you."

"You might if you managed well, because I am a rich man. But you are sure to bungle."

He turned to the woman and asked with great kindness:

"Is it their first crime?"

"Yes, sir," she said. "Mr.——"

"Shut up!" growled one of her companions.

"A gentleman from New York turned us out of the woods so's he could have them all to himself and after we'd spent all our money on lawyers. So my husband and the boys allowed they had about enough of the law. And so they held up the express, but it was more because they were mad clear through than because they are bad, and now it's too late, and—and——"

Here she began to cry.

"It's never too late to mend," said Maud.

"Have you spent any of the money they took?" asked Colonel Meredith.

"No, sir; we haven't had a chance. We've got every dime of it."

The Seven Darlings

"Did you own the land you were driven off?"

"No, sir, but we'd always lived on it, and it did seem as if we ought to be left in peace——"

"To shoot out of season, to burn other people's wood, trap their fish, and show your teeth at them when they came to take what belonged to them? I congratulate you. You are American to the backbone. And now you propose to take my money away from me."

Colonel Meredith turned to his cousin, after excusing himself to Maud, and they conversed for some time in their strange Sea Island dialect.

"Can that gibberish," said one of the train robbers suddenly. "I'm sick of it."

"We shan't trouble you with it again, as we've already decided what to do."

The robber laughed mockingly.

"In view of your extreme youth," said Colonel Meredith sweetly, "in view of the fact that you are also young in crime and that one member of your party is a woman, we have decided to help you along the road to reform. In my State there is considerable lawlessness; from this has evolved the useful custom of going heeled."

He spoke, and a blue automatic flashed cruelly in his white hand. His action was as sudden and unexpected as the striking of a rattlesnake.

The Seven Darlings

"All hands up," he commanded.

There was a long silence.

"You've got us," said the youngest of the robbers sheepishly. "How about the man on guard with a Winchester?"

"My cousin Mr. Jonstone will bring him in to join the conference. And, meanwhile, I shall have to ask the ladies to look the other way while my cousin changes clothes with one of you gentlemen."

Of the three villains, Jonstone selected the youngest and the tidiest, and with mutual reluctance, suspicion, and startled glances toward where the ladies sat with averted faces, they changed clothes.

A broad felt hat, several sizes too big for him, added the touch of completion to the Carolinian's transformation. He took the spare Winchester and, without a word, walked quietly toward the mouth of the cave and was lost to sight.

Maud did not breathe freely until he had returned, unhurt, carrying both Winchesters and driving an exceedingly sheepish backwoodsman before him.

He expressed the wish to resume his own clothes. This done, he and his cousin broke into good-natured, boyish laughter.

The Seven Darlings

The oldest and most sheepish of the backwoods-men kept repeating, "Who would 'a' thought he'd have a pistol on him!" and seemed to find a world of comfort in the thought.

"What are you going to do with them?" Maud asked almost in a whisper. "I think I feel a little sorry for them."

"Bob!" exclaimed Colonel Meredith.

"What?"

"*She* feels a little sorry for them. Don't you?"

"Yes, *sir!*" replied Mr. Jonstone fervently.

Colonel Meredith addressed himself to the young woman with the old face.

"Do you believe in fairies?" he asked.

She only looked pathetic and confused.

"Miss Darling, here," he went on, "is a fairy. She left her wand at home, but if she wants to she can make people's wishes come true. Now suppose you and your friends talk things over and decide upon some sensible wishes to have granted. Of course, it's no use wishing you hadn't robbed a train; but you could wish that the money would be returned, and that the police could be induced to stop looking for you, and that some one could come along and offer you an honest way of making a living. So you talk it over a while and then tell us what you'd like."

The Seven Darlings

"Aren't you going to give us up?" asked one of the men.

"Not if you've any sense at all."

"Then I guess there's no use us talking things over. And if the young lady is a fairy, we'd be obliged if she'd get busy along the lines you've just laid down."

All eyes were turned on Maud. And she looked appealingly from Colonel Meredith to Mr. Jonstone and back again.

"What ought I to say? What ought I to promise? *Can* the money be returned? Can the police be called off? And if I only had some work to give them, but over at The Camp——"

"Every good fairy," said Colonel Meredith, "has two helpers to whom all things are possible."

"Truly?"

The Carolinians sprang to their feet, clicked their heels together into the first position of dancing, laid their right hands over their hearts, and bowed very low.

"Then," said Maud laughing, "I should like the money to be returned."

"I will attend to that," said Colonel Meredith.

"And the police to be called off."

Again the soldier assumed responsibility.

The Seven Darlings

"But who," she asked, "will find work for them?"

"I will," said Mr. Jonstone. "They shall build the house for my cousin and me to live in. You can build a house, can't you? A log house?"

"But where will you build it?" asked Maud. "You found fault with all the best sites on the lake."

"The very first site we visited suited us to perfection."

"But you said the spring contained cyanide or something."

"We were talking through our hats."

"But why——"

The Carolinians gazed at her with a kind of beseeching ardor, until she understood that they had only found fault with one promising building site after another in order that they might pass the longest time possible in her company.

And she returned their glance with one in which there was some feeling stronger than mere amusement.

XXIV

CONCERNING information, Mark Twain wrote that it appeared to stew out of him naturally, like the precious ottar of roses out of the otter. With the narrator of this episodical history, however, things are very different. And just how the good fairy, Maud Darling, was enabled to keep her promises to the outlaws seems to him of no great moment. But the money *was* returned to the express company; the police *were* called off; and the four robbers, with the woman to cook for them, went to work at building a log house on the point of pines to be occupied in the near future by the Carolinians.

They were not sorry to have been turned from a life of sin. It is only when a life of sin is gilded, padded, and pleasant that people hate to turn from it. When virtue entails being rained on, starved, and hunted, it isn't a very pleasant way of life, either.

The face of the young female bandit lost its look of premature old age. She went about her work singing, and the humming of the kettle was

The Seven Darlings

her accompaniment. The four men looked the other men of the camp in the face and showed how to lay trees by the heels in record time. To their well-swung and even better-sharpened axes even the stems of oaks were as wax candles. It became quite "the thing" for guests at The Camp to go out to the point and admire the axe-work and all the processes of frontier house-building.

When people speak of "love in a cottage," there rises nearly always, in my mind, the memory of a log house that a friend of mine and I came across by the headwaters of a great river in Canada.

It stood—the axe marks crisp, white, and blistered with pitch—upon the brink of a swirling brown pool full of grilse. The logs of which it was built had been dragged from a distance, so that in the immediate neighborhood of the cabin was no desolation of dead tree-tops and dying stumps. Everything was wonderfully neat, new, and in order. About the pool and the cabin the maples had turned yellow and vermilion. And above was the peaceful pale blue of an Indian-summer sky.

We opened the door, held by a simple latch, and found ourselves in the pleasantest of rooms, just twenty feet by fifteen. The walls and the floor had been much whitened and smoothed by the axe. The place smelt vaguely of pitch and strongly of balsam. There was a fireplace— the fire all laid, a bunk to lie on, a chair to sit on, a table to write on, a broom to sweep with. And neatly set upon clean shelves were various jams in glass, and meats, biscuits, and soups in tins. There was also a writing (on birch bark) over the shelves, which read: "Help yourself."

We took down the shutters from the windows and let in floods of autumn sun. Then we lighted the fire, and ate crackers and jam.

It hurt a little to learn at the mouth of our guide that the cabin belonged to a somewhat notorious and decidedly crotchety New York financier who controlled the salmon-fishing in those waters. I had pictured it as built for a pair of eminently sensible and supernaturally romantic honeymooners or for a poet. And I wanted to carry away that impression. For in such a place love or inspiration must have lasted just as long as the crackers and jam. And there is no more to be said of a palace.

One day Mary Darling and Sam Langham visited the new cabin. And Sam said: "If one of the happy pair happened to know something of cooking, what a place for a honeymoon!"

Shortly afterward, Phyllis and Herring came

that way, and Herring said: "If I was in love, and knew how to use an axe, I'd build just such a house for the girl I love and make her live in it. I believe I will, anyway."

"Believe what?" asked Phyllis demurely. "Believe you will make her live in it?"

"Yes," he said darkly—"no matter who she is and no matter how afraid of the mice and spiders with which such places ultimately become infested."

Lee and Renier visited the cabin, also. They remarked only that it had a wonderfully smooth floor, and proceeded at once thereon, Lee whistling exquisitely and with much spirit, to dance a maxixe, which was greatly admired by the ex-outlaws.

Maud came often with the Carolinians, and as for Eve, she came once or twice all by herself.

Jealousy is a horrid passion. It had never occurred to Eve Darling that she was or ever could be jealous of anybody. And she wasn't—exactly. But seeing her sisters always cavaliered by attractive men and slipping casually into thrilling and even dangerous adventures with them disturbed the depths of her equanimity. It was delightful, of course, to be made much of by Arthur and to go upon excursions with him

The Seven Darlings

as of old. But something was wanting. Arthur's idea of a pleasant day in the woods was to sit for hours by a pool and attempt to classify the croaks of frogs, or to lie upon his back in the sun and think about the girl in far-off China whom he loved so hopelessly.

Thanks to her excellent subordinate, and to her own administrative ability, Laundry House made fewer and fewer encroachments upon Eve's leisure. And often she found that time was hanging upon her hands with great heaviness. Memory reminded her that things had not always been thus; for there are men in this world who think that she was the most beautiful of all the Darlings.

It was curious that of all the men who had come to The Camp, Mr. Bob Jonstone had the most attraction for her. They had not spoken half a dozen times, and it was quite obvious that his mind, if not his heart, was wholly occupied with Maud. Wherever you saw Maud, you could be pretty sure that the Carolinians, hunting in a couple, were not far off. Of the two, Colonel Meredith was the more brilliant, the more showy, and the better-looking. Added to his good breeding and lazy, pleasant voice were certain Yankee qualities—a total lack of gullibility, a

233

certain trace of mockery, even upon serious sub-
jects. Mr. Jonstone, on the other hand, was a
perfect lamb of earnestness and sincerity. If he
heard of an injustice his eyes flamed, or if he
listened to the recital of some pathetic happening
they misted over. Once beyond the direct influence of his cousin there was neither mischief
in him nor devilment. It was for this reason, and
in this knowledge, that he had put his newly ac-
quired moneys in trust for himself.

In the little house by the lake where the cousins
still slept, conversation seldom flagged before one
or two o'clock in the morning. Having said good-
night to each other at about eleven, one or the
other was pretty sure to let out some new discovery about the Darlings in general and Maud
Darling in particular, and then all desire for sleep
vanished and their real cousinly confidences began.

But these confidences had their limits, for
neither confessed to being sentimentally interested in the young lady, whereas, within limits,
they both were. And each enjoyed the satisfaction of believing (quite erroneously) that he deceived the other. I do not wish to convey the
impression that they were actually in love with
her.

When you are really in love, you are also in

The Seven Darlings

love before breakfast. That is the final test. And
when love begins to die, that is the time when its
weakening pulse is first to be concerned. What
honest man has not been mad about some pretty
girl (in a crescendo of madness) from tea time till
sleep time and waked in the morning with no
thought but for toast and coffee the soonest possible? and gone about the business of the morning and early afternoon almost heart-whole and
fancy-free, and relapsed once more into madness
with the lengthening of the shadows? A man
who proposes marriage to a girl until he has been
in love with her for twenty-four consecutive
hours is a light fellow who ought to be kicked out
of the house by her papa. As for the girl, let her
be sure that he is bread and meat to her, comfort
and rest, demigod and man, wholly necessary
and not to be duplicated in this world, before she
even says that she will think about it.

In the early morning there would arise in the
house of the Carolinians the sounds of whistling,
of singing, laughter, scuffling, and running water.
So that a girl who really wanted either of them
must, in listening, have despaired.

As for Maud Darling, she was disgusted with
herself—theoretically. But practically she was
having the time of her life. In theory, she felt

The Seven Darlings

that no self-respecting girl ought to be unable to decide which of the two young men she liked the better. In practice, she found a constant pondering of this delicate question to be delightful. It was very comfortable to know that the moment she was free to play there were two pleasant companions ready and waiting.

Sentiment and gayety attended their goings and comings. The Carolinians, fortified by each other's presence, were veritable Raleighs of extravagant devotion. In engineering, for instance, so that Maud should not have to step in a damp place, there were displayed enough gallantry and efficiency to have saved her from an onslaught of tigers. If the trio climbed a mountain, Maud gave herself up to the heart-warming delight of being helped when help was not in the least necessary. In short, she behaved as any natural young woman would, and should. She flirted outrageously. But in the depths of her heart a genuine friendship for the Carolinians was conceived and grew in breadth and strength. What if they did out-gallant gallantry?

XXV

ONE Sunday, Eve, from her window—she
was rather a lazy girl that Sunday—wit-
nessed the following departures from the camp.
Sam Langham and Mary in a guide boat, with
fishing-tackle and an immense hamper which
looked like lunch. Herring and Phyllis could be
seen hoisting the sails on the knockabout. Herring
had never sailed a boat and was prepared to master that simple art at once. Lee and Renier were
girt for the mountain. Renier appeared to have
a Flobert rifle in semihiding under his coat, and
it was to be feared that if he saw a partridge, he
would open fire on it, close season though it was.
He and Lee would justify this illegal act by cooking the bird for their lunch. Gay commandeered
the *Streak* and departed at high speed toward
Carrytown. She had in one hand a sheet of blue-
striped paper, folded. It resembled a cablegram.
And Eve thought that it must be of a very private nature, or else Gay would have telephoned
it to the Western Union office, instead of carrying
it by hand. The next to depart from the camp

The Seven Darlings

was Arthur. He moved dreamily in a north-westerly direction, accompanied by Uncas, the chipmunk, and Wow, the dog. Other guests made departures.

All of which Eve, half dressed and looking lazily from her window, lazily noted, remarking that for her Sunday was a day of rest and that she thanked Heaven for it. And she did not feel any differently until Maud and the Carolinians walked out on the float and began to pack a guide boat for the day.

Then her lazy, complacent feelings departed, and were succeeded by a sudden, wide-awake surge of self-pity. She felt like Cinderella. Nobody had asked her to go anywhere or do anything, and nobody had even thought of doing so. When she was dead they would gather round her coffin and remember that they hadn't asked her to go anywhere or do anything, and they would be very sorry and ashamed and they would say what a nice girl she had been, and how she had always tried to give everybody a good time.

Between laughter and tears and mortification, Eve finished dressing, set her lovely jaw, and went out into the delicious, cool calm of the mountain morning. She could still hear the voices of many of the departing ones; and the

She felt like Cinderella. Nobody had asked her to go anywhere
or do anything

The Seven Darlings

rattling and creaking of the knockabout's blocks and rigging. She heard Herring say to Phyllis: "I think it would be better if I could make the boom go out on this side, but I can't." Phyllis's answer was a cool, contented laugh. It was as if she said: "Hang the boom! *We're* here!"

Have you ever had the feeling that you would like to board a swift boat, head for the open sea, and never come back? Or that you could plunge into some boundless, trackless forest and keep straight on until you were lost, and died (beautifully and painlessly), and were covered with beautiful leaves by little birds?

Eve enjoyed (and suffered from) a hint of this latter feeling. She ate a light breakfast (it would be better not to begin starving till she was actually lost in the boundless, trackless forest), selected a light, spiked climbing-stick with a crooked handle, headed for one of the northeasterly mountains, and was soon deep in the shade of the pines and hemlocks.

After a few miles, the trail that she followed split and scattered in many directions, like the end of an unravelled rope. She followed an old lumber road for a long way, turned into another that crossed it at an angle of forty-five degrees, took no account of the sun's position in the heavens

239

or of the marked sides of trees. If she came to a high place from which there was a view, she did not look at it. She just kept going—this way and that, up and down. In short, she made a conscious, anxious effort to lose herself. The easterly mountain toward which she had first headed kept bobbing up straight ahead. And always there was the knowledge in the back of her head of the exact location of The Camp, and of all the other landmarks, familiar to her since early youth.

"Drag it!" she said, at length, her eyes on the mountain. "I'll climb the old thing, put melancholy aside, and call this a good, if unaccompanied, Sunday."

The morning coolness had departed. It was one of those hot, breathless, mountain forenoons that kill the appetite and are usually followed, toward the late afternoon, by violent electrical disturbances.

Eve was not as fit as she had supposed, or as she thought. As a matter of fact, she was setting too fast a pace, considering the weather and the angle of the mountain slope; and she was as wet as if she had played several hard sets of tennis with a partner who stood in one corner of the court and let her do all the running.

The Seven Darlings

As she climbed, reproaching her wind for being so short, she remembered that the hollow tip of this particular northeastern mountain was filled with a deep pool of water. Nobody had ever called it a lake. The map called it a pond; but it wasn't even that—it was a pool. Springs fed it just fast enough to make up for the evaporation. It had no outlet. It was shaped like a fat letter O. At one end was a little beach of white sand. Indeed, the bottom of the pool was all firm, smooth, and clean, and the whole charming little body of water was surrounded by thick groves of dwarf mountain trees and bushes. Not content with being a perfect replica, in miniature, of a full-grown Adirondack lake, this pool had in its midst an island, a dozen feet in diameter, densely shrubbed and shaded by one diminutive Japanesque pine.

When Eve came to the pool, hot, tired, and rather bothered at the thought of the long walk back to camp, she had but the vaguest idea of just why the Lord had placed such a pool on top of a mountain, impelled her to climb that mountain, and made the day so piping hot.

Eve stood a little on the sand beach. She felt hotter and hotter, and the pool looked cooler and cooler. Presently, a heavenly smile of solution brightened her flushed, warm face, and she with-

The Seven Darlings

drew into a shady clump of bushes. From this there came first the exclamation "Drag it!" then a sound of some sort of a string being sharply broken in two, and then there came from the clump of bushes Eve herself, looking for all the world like a slice of the silver moon.

And as you may have seen the silver moon slip slowly into the sea, so Eve vanished slowly into the pool—all but her shapely little round head, with its crisp bright-brown hair and its lovely face, happy now, exhilarated, and eager as are the faces of adventurers.

And Eve thought if one didn't have to eat, if one didn't end by being cold, if one could make time stand still—she would choose to be always and forever a slice of the silver moon, lolling in a mountain pool.

She had the kind of hair that wets to perfection. But it was not the sort of permanent wave which lasts six months or so, costs twenty-five dollars, and is inculcated by hours of alternate baking and shampooing. Eve had always had a permanent wave. She feared neither fog nor rain, nor water in any form of application. And so it was that, now and then, as she lolled about the pool, she disappeared from one fortunate square yard of surface and reappeared in another.

The Seven Darlings

Half an hour had passed, when suddenly the mountain stillness was broken by men's voices.

Eve was at the opposite side of the pool from where she had left her clothes. Between her and the approaching voices was the little island. She landed hastily upon this and hid herself among the bushes.

Three gross, fat men and one long, lean man, with a face like leather and an Adam's apple that bobbed like a fisherman's float, came down to the beach, sweating terribly, and cast thereon knapsacks, picnic baskets, hatchets, fishing-tackle, and all the complicated paraphernalia of amateurs about to cook their own lunch in the woods.

All but one had loud, coarse, carrying voices, and they all appeared to belong to the ruling class. They appeared, in short, to have neither education nor refinement nor charm nor anything to commend them as leaders or examples. Eve wondered how it was possible for them to find pleasure even in each other's company. They quarrelled, wrangled, found fault, abused each other, or suddenly forgot their differences, gathering about the fattest of the fat men and listening, almost reverently, while he told a story. When he had finished, they would throw their heads far back and scream with laughter. He must have told wonderfully funny stories; but his voice was no more than a husky whisper, so that Eve could not make head or tail of them.

After a while the whispering fat man produced from one of the baskets four little glasses and a fat dark bottle. And shortly after there was less wrangling and more laughter.

The thin man with the leathery face and the bobbing Adam's apple put a fishing-rod together, tied a couple of gaudy flies to his leader, and began to cast most unskilfully from the shores of the pool, moving along slowly from time to time.

The fat men, occasionally calling to ask if he had caught anything, busied themselves with preparations for lunch. One of them made tremendous chopping sounds in the wood and furnished from time to time incommensurate supplies of fire-wood. Smoke arose and a kettle was slung.

Meanwhile Eve, cowering among the bushes, for all the world like her famous ancestress when the angel came to the garden, did not quite know what to do. She had only to lift her voice and explain, and the men would go away for a time. She felt sure of that. She had been brought up

Eve was at the opposite side of the pool from where she had left
her clothes

The Seven Darlings

to believe in the exquisite chivalry of the plain American man.

But there was something about the four which repelled her, · which stuck in her throat. She did not wish to be under any sort of obligation to any of them. And so she kept mousy-quiet, and turned over in her mind an immense number of worthless stratagems and expedients.

Have you ever tried to lie on the lawn under a tree and read for an hour or two—incased in all your buffer of clothes? Try it some time—without the buffers. Try it in the buff. And then imagine how comfortable Eve was on the island. Imagine how soft it felt to her elbows, for instance. And imagine to yourself, too, that it was not an uninhabited island—but one upon which an immense gray spider had made a home and raised a family.

From time to time the inept caster of flies returned to the camp-fire, always in answer to a boisterous summons from his friends. And after each visit, his leathery face became redder and his casting more absurd.

Finally his flies caught in a tree, his rod broke, and he abandoned the gentle art of angling for that time and place. Meanwhile steam ran from the kettle and mingled with the smoke of the

The Seven Darlings

fire. The sound of voices was incessant. Ten minutes later the gentlemen were served.

Midway of the meal, some of which was burnt black and some of which was quite raw, there was produced a thermos bottle as big as the leg of a rubber boot. And a moment later, icy-cold champagne was frothing and bubbling in tumblers.

In that high air, upon a thick foundation of raw whiskey, the brilliant wine of France had soon built a triumphant edifice, so that Eve, cold now, miserable, and frightened, felt that the time for an appeal to chivalry was long since past.

Far from their wives and constituents, the four politicians were obviously not going to stop short of complete drunkenness. Indeed, it was an opportunity hardly to be missed. For where else in the woods could nature be more exquisite, dignified, and inspiring?

It got so that Eve could no longer bear to watch them or to listen to them. Pink with shame, fury, hatred, and fear, she stuffed her fingers in her ears and hid her face.

Thus lying, there came to her after quite a long interval, dimly, a shout and a howl of laughter with an entirely new intonation. She looked up then and saw the thin man, waist-deep in the

The Seven Darlings

bushes, just where she had left her clothes, making faces of beastly mystery at his companions, beckoning to them and urging them to come look. They went to him, presently, staggering and evil.

And then they scattered and began to hunt for her.

XXVI

"TIRED?" queried Mr. Bob Jonstone, with some indignation. "I'm not a bit tired. I haven't had enough exercise to keep me quiet. And if it wasn't your turn to make the fire, your privilege, and your prerogative, I'd insist on chopping the wood myself. No," he said, leaning back luxuriously, "I find it very hard to keep still. This walking on the level is child's play. What I need to keep me in good shape is mountains to climb."

"Like those we have at home," said Colonel Meredith, and if he didn't actually wink at Maud, who was arranging some chops on a broiler, he made one eye smaller than the other.

"What's wrong with *this* mountain?" asked Maud.

"Why, we are only half-way up, and the real view is from the top!"

"Of course," said Colonel Meredith, "if you want to see the view, don't let us stop you. We'll wait for you. Won't we, Miss Maud?"

She nodded, her eyes shining with mischief.

248

The Seven Darlings

"But," the colonel continued, "Bob is a bluff. He's had all the climbing he can stand. Nothing but a chest full of treasure or a maiden in distress would take him a step farther."

"After lunch," said Mr. Jonstone, "I shall."

"Do it now! Lunch won't be ready for an hour. Any kind of a walker could make the top of the mountain and be back in that time. But I'll bet you anything you like that you can't."

"You will? I'll bet you fifty dollars."

"Done!"

Mr. Jonstone leaped to his feet in a business-like way, waved his hand to them, and started briskly off and up along the trail by which they had come, and which ended only at the very top of the mountain. It wasn't that he wanted any more exercise. He wanted to get away for a while to think things over. He had learned on that day's excursion, or thought he had, that two is company and that three isn't. The pleasant interchangeableness of the trio's relations seemed suddenly to have undergone a subtle change. It was as if Maud and Colonel Meredith had suddenly found that they liked each other a little better than they liked him.

So it wasn't a man in search of exercise or eager to win a bet who was hastening toward the top of a mountain, but a child who had just discovered that dolls are stuffed with sawdust. He suffered a little from jealousy, and a little from anger. He could not have specified what they had done to him that morning, and it may have been his imagination alone that was to blame, but they had made him feel, or he had made himself feel, like a guest who is present, not because he is wanted but because for some reason or other he had to be asked.

He walked himself completely out of breath and that did his mind good. Resting before making a final spurt to the mountain-top, he heard men's voices shouting and hallooing in the forest. The sounds carried him back to certain coon and rabbit hunts in his native State, and he wondered what these men could be hunting. And having recovered his breath, he went on.

He came suddenly in view of a great round pool of water in the midst of which was a tiny island, thickly wooded. Just in front of him a fire burned low on a beach of white sand.

Upon the beach, his back to Jonstone, stood a tall, thin man who appeared to be gazing at the island. Suddenly this man began to shout aloud:

"She's on the island! She's on the island!"

From the woods came the sound of crashings,

scramblings, and oaths, and, one by one, three fat men, very sweaty and crimson in the face, came reeling out on the beach, and ranged themselves with the thin man, and looked drunkenly toward the island.

"She's hiding on the island, the cute thing," said the thin man.

"Did you see her?"

"I saw the bushes move. That's where she is."

"How deep's the water?"

"I'll tell you in about a minute," said the thin man. He threw his coat from him, and, sitting down with a sudden lurch, began to unlace his boots.

"Maybe you don't know it," he said, "but I'm some swimmer, I am."

There was a moment of silence and then there came from the island a voice that sent a thrill through Mr. Bob Jonstone from head to foot. The voice was like frightened music with a sob in it.

"Won't you please go away!"

"Good God," he thought, "they're hunting a woman!"

The drunken men had answered that sobbing appeal with a regular view-halloo of drunken laughter.

Mr. Bob Jonstone stepped slowly forward. His

thin face had a bluish, steely look; and his eyes glinted wickedly like a rattlesnake's. Being one against four, he made no declaration of war. He came upon them secretly from behind. And first he struck a thin neck just below a leathery ear, and then a fat neck.

He was not a strong man physically. But high-strung nerves and cold, collected loathing and fury are powerful weapons.

The thin man and the fat man with the whispering voice lay face down on the beach and passed from insensibility into stupefied, drunken sleep. But with the other two, Mr. Jonstone had a bad time of it, for he had broken a bone in his right hand and the pain was excruciating. Often, during that battle, he thought of the deadly automatic in his pocket. But if he used that, it meant that a woman's name would be printed in the newspaper.

The fat men fought hard with drunken fury. Their strength was their weight, and they were always coming at him from opposite sides. But an empty whiskey bottle caught Mr. Jonstone's swift eye and made a sudden end of what its contents had begun. He hit five times and then stood alone, among the fallen, a bottle neck of brown glass in his hand.

"I don't want you to see me, if you don't mind. I don't want you to know who I am. But I'm the gratefulest girl that ever lived"

The Seven Darlings

Then he lifted his voice and spoke aloud, as if
to the island:

"They'll not trouble you now. What else
can I do?"

"God bless you for doing what you've done!
I'm a fool girl, and I thought I was all alone and
I went in swimming, and they came and I hid
on the island. And I—I haven't got my things
with me!"

"Couldn't you get ashore without being seen?
These beasts won't look. And I won't look.
You can trust me, can't you?"

"When you tell me that nobody is looking I'll
come ashore."

"Nobody is looking now."

He heard a splash and sounds as of strong
swimming. And he was dying to look. He took
out his little automatic and cocked it, and he said
to himself: "If you do look, Bob, you get shot."

Ten minutes passed.

"Are you all right?" he called.

"Yes, thank you, all right now. But how can
I thank you? I don't want you to see me, if you
don't mind. I don't want you to know who I
am. But I'm the gratefulest girl that ever lived;
and I'm going home now, wiser than when I
came, and, listen——"

The Seven Darlings

"I'm listening."

"I think I'd almost die for you. There!"

Mr. Jonstone's hair fairly bristled with emotion.

"But am I never to see you, never to know your name?"

The answer came from farther off.

"Yes, I think so. Some time."

"Do you promise that?"

Silence—and then:

"I *almost* promise."

.   .   .   .

Having assured himself that the drunken men were not dead, Mr. Jonstone sighed like a furnace and started down the mountain.

His hand hurt him like the devil, but the pain was first cousin to delight.

XXVII

THE Camp was much concerned to hear of poor Mr. Jonstone's accident. A round stone, he said, had rolled suddenly under his foot and precipitated him down a steep pitch of path. He had put out his hands to save his face and, it seemed, broken a bone in one of them. And at that, the attempted rescue of his face had not been an overwhelming success.

It was not until the doctor had come and gone that Mr. Jonstone told his cousin what had really happened. Colonel Meredith was much excited and intrigued by the narrative.

"And you've no idea who she was?" he asked.

"No, Mel; I've thought that the voice was familiar. I've thought that it wasn't. It was a very well-bred Northern voice—but agitated probably out of its natural intonations. Voices are queer things. A man might not recognize his own mother's voice at a time when he was not expecting to hear it."

"Voices," said Colonel Meredith, "are beautiful things. This wasn't a motherly sort of voice, was it?"

The Seven Darlings

"But it might be," said Mr. Jonstone gently.
"I wonder if they've anything in this place to
make a fellow sleep. Bromide isn't much good
when you've a sure-enough sharp pain."

"You feel mighty uncomfortable, don't you,
Bob?"

The invalid nodded. He was pale as a sheet,
and he could not keep still. He had received
considerable physical punishment and his entire
nervous system was quivering and jumping.

"I'll see if anybody's got anything," said
Colonel Meredith, and he went straight to the
office, where he found Maud Darling and Eve.

"My cousin is feeling like the deuce," he said.
"He won't sleep all night if we don't give him
something to make him. Do you know of any
one that's got anything of that sort—morphine,
for instance?"

"The best thing will be to take the *Streak* and
get some from the doctor," said Maud. "Let's
all go."

"I think I won't," said Eve, looking wonderfully cool and serene. "But I'll walk down to
the float and see you off. What a pity for a man
to get laid up by an accident that might have
been avoided by a little attention!"

Colonel Meredith stiffened.

The Seven Darlings

"I am sorry to contradict a lady," he said, "but my cousin has given me the particulars of his accident, and it was of a nature that could hardly have been avoided by a man. I think, Miss Maud, if you will order a launch, I had better tell my cousin where I am going, in case he should feel that he was being neglected."

"Don't bother to do that," said Eve. "I'll get word to him."

"Oh, thank you so much, will you?"

"He's lying down, I suppose."

"Yes; he has retired for the night."

"I'll send one of the men," said Eve, "or Sam Langham."

So they went one way and Eve went the other, walking very quickly and smiling in the night.

"Mr. Jonstone—oh, Mr. Jonstone! Can you hear me?"

With a sort of shudder of wonder Mr. Jonstone sat up in his bed.

"Yes," he said, "I do hear you—unless I am dreaming."

"You're not dreaming. You are in great pain, owing to an accident which could hardly have been avoided by a man, and can't sleep."

"I am in no pain now."

"Colonel, Meredith has gone to Carrytown for

something to make you sleep, so you aren't to
fret and feel neglected if he doesn't come back
to you at once."

"Just the same it's a horrible feeling—to be
all alone."

"But if some one—any one were to stay within
call—— ?"

"If *you* were to stay within call it would make
all the difference in the world."

"You don't know who I am, do you?"

"I don't know what you look like, and I don't
know your name. But I know who you are.
And once upon a time—long years ago—you
promised, you half promised, to tell me the other
things."

"My name is a very, very old name, and I look
like a lot of other people. But you say you know
who I am. Who am I?"

Mr. Bob Jonstone laughed softly.

"It's enough," said he, "that I know. But
are you comfortable out there? You're on the
porch, aren't you?"

"No; I'm standing on the ground and resting
my lazy forehead against the porch railing."

"I'd feel easier if you came on the porch and
made yourself comfortable in a chair, just outside my window. And we could talk easier."

The Seven Darlings

"But you're not supposed to talk."

"Listening would be good for me."

There was a sound of light steps and of a chair being dragged.

"I wish you wouldn't sit just round the corner," said Mr. Jonstone presently. "If you sat before the window, sideways, I could see your profile against the sky."

"I'm doing very well where I am, thank you."

"But, please, why shouldn't I see you? Why are you so embarrassed at me?"

"Wouldn't you be embarrassed if you were a girl and had been through the adventure I went through? Wouldn't you be a little embarrassed to see the man who helped you, and look him in the face?"

"Don't you ever want me to see you? Because, if you don't, I will go away from this place in the morning and never come back."

"Somehow, that doesn't appeal to me very much either."

"I am glad," said Mr. Jonstone quietly.

"How does your hand feel?"

"Which hand?"

"The one you hurt."

"It feels very happy, and the other hand feels very jealous of it."

The Seven Darlings

"Seriously—are you having a pretty bad time?"

"I am having the time of my life—seriously—the time that lucky men always have once in their lives."

"Are you very impatient for the morphine?"

"I shall not take it when it comes. It is far better knowing what one knows, remembering what one remembers, and looking forward to what a presumptuous fool cannot help but look forward to—it is far better to keep awake; to lie peacefully in the dark, knowing, remembering, and looking forward."

"And just what are you looking forward to?"

"To a long life and a happy one; to the sounds of a voice; to a sudden coming to life of the whole 'Oxford Book of Verse'; to seeing a face."

There was a long silence.

"Are you there?"

"Yes; but you mustn't talk."

"I think you are tired. Please don't stay any more if you are tired."

"I'm not tired."

"Then perhaps you are bored."

"I'm not bored."

"Then what are you?"

"You keep quiet."

The Seven Darlings

When, at last, Colonel Meredith came, important with morphine and the doctor's instructions, he found his cousin Mr. Bob Jonstone sleeping very quietly and peacefully, a much dog-eared copy of the "Oxford Book of Verse" clasped to his breast.

Unfortunately the colonel, after putting out the light again, bumped into a table, and Mr. Jonstone waked.

"That you, Mel?"

"Yes, Bob; sorry I waked you. Did Miss Darling send word explaining that I should be quite a while coming back?"

"Which Miss Darling?"

"Which? Why, Miss Eve."

"Yes, she sent word."

"And how have you been?"

"I took a turn for the better shortly after you left. A little while ago I lighted a candle, and read a little and got sleepy. And now I think I'll go to sleep again."

"You don't need the morphine?"

"No, Mel. Thank you. Good-night."

"Good-night."

"Mel?"

"What is it?"

"Isn't Eve about the oldest name you know?"

The Seven Darlings

"Oldest, I guess, except Adam and Lilith. You go to sleep."

And Colonel Meredith tiptoed out of the room, murmuring: "Seems to be a little shaky in his upper stories."

XXVIII

A POINT of land just across the lake from the
camp belonged to the Darlings' mother,
the Princess Oducalchi. One night the light of
fires and lanterns appeared on this point and the
next morning it was seen to be studded here and
there with pale-brown tents. The Darlings were
annoyed to think that any one should trespass on
so large a scale on some one else's land. In a code
of laws shot to pieces with class legislation, trespassers are, of course, exempt from punishment;
their presence and depredations in one's private
melon-patch are none the less disagreeable, and
Arthur Darling, as his mother's representative,
was peculiarly enraged.

Arthur, in his idle moments, when, for instance,
he was not studying the webs of spiders or clas-
sifying the cries of frogs, sometimes let his mind
run on politics and the whole state of the Union.
In such matters, of course, he was only a tyro.
Why should the puny and prejudiced population
of Texas have two votes in the Senate when
the hordes of New York have but two ? Why, in

The Seven Darlings

a popular form of government, should the minority do the ruling? Why should not a hardworking rich man have an equal place in the sun with a man who, through laziness and a moral nature twisted like a pretzel, remains poor? Why should education be forced on children in a country where education, which means good manners and the ability to distinguish between right and wrong, amounts practically to disfranchisement?

Arthur, in his political ruminations, could never get beyond such questions as these. If A has paid for and owns a piece of land, why is it not A's to enjoy, rather than B's, whose sole claim thereto is greater strength of body than A, and the desire to possess those things which are not his?

At least, Arthur could row across to the point and protest in his mother's name. If the trespassers were gentlefolk who imagined themselves to have camped upon public land, they would, of course, offer to go and to pay all damages—in which event, Arthur would invite them to stay as long as they pleased, only begging that they would not set the woods on fire. If, however, the trespassers belonged to one of the privileged classes for whose benefit the laws are made and continued, he would simply be abused roundly and perhaps vilely. He would then take a thrashing at the

264

The Seven Darlings

hands of superior numbers, and the incident would be closed.

Colonel Meredith, seeing Arthur about to embark on his mission, offered help and comfort in the emergency.

"Just you wait till I fetch my rifle," he said; "and if there's any trifling, we'll shoot them up."

"Shoot them up!" exclaimed Arthur. "If we shot them up, we'd go from here to prison and from prison to the electric chair."

"In South Carolina," Colonel Meredith protested, "if a man comes on our land and we tell him to get off and he won't, we drill a hole in him."

"And that's one of the best things about the South," said Arthur. "But we do things differently in the North. If a man comes on my land and I tell him to get off and he says he won't, then I have the right to put him off, using as much force as is necessary. And if he is twice as big as I am and there are three or four of him, you can see, without using glasses, how the matter must end."

"Then all you are out for is to take a licking?"

"That is my only privilege under the law. But I hope I shall not have to avail myself of it. Where there are so many tents there must be

money. Where there is money there are possessions, and where there are possessions, there are
the same feelings about property that you and I
have."

"Still," said Colonel Meredith, "I wish you'd
take me along and our guns. There is always the
chance of managing matters so that fatalities may
be construed into acts of self-defense."

"Get behind me, you man of blood!" exclaimed
Arthur, laughing, and he leaped into a canoe, and
with a part of the same impulse sent it flying far
out from the float. Then, standing, he started
for the brown tents with easy, powerful strokes,
very earnest for the speedy accomplishment of
a disagreeable duty. That anything really pleasant might come of his expedition never entered
his head.

"Arthur gone to put them off?"

"Why, yes! Good-morning, Miss Gay."

"Good-morning, yourself, Colonel Meredith,
and many of them. Want to look?"

"Thank you."

Colonel Meredith focussed the glasses upon the
brown tents.

"What do you make them out to be?"

"I can make out a sort of nigger carrying tea
into one of the tents. And there's a young lady

"He's paddling as if he expected to cross a hundred yards of water in
a second"

in black. She seems to be walking down to the shore to meet your brother. And now she's waving her hand to him."

"The impudent thing," exclaimed Gay. "What's my brother doing?"

"He's paddling as if he expected to cross a hundred yards of water in a second. If the young lady comes any closer to the water, she'll get wet."

Suddenly blushing crimson, he thrust the field-glasses back into Gay's hands, and cried with complete conviction that he was "blessed."

In the bright field of magnification, hastily focussed to her own vision, Gay beheld her brother and the young woman in black tightly locked in each other's arms.

XXIX

TO Arthur, half-way across the lake, considering just what he should say to the trespassers, the sudden sight of the person whom of all persons in the world he least expected and most wanted to see was a staggering physical shock. He almost fell out of his canoe. And if he had done that he might very likely have drowned, so paralyzing in effect were those first moments of unbelievable joy and astonishment. Then she waved her hand to him and swiftly crossed the beach, and he began to paddle like a madman. When the canoe beached with sudden finality, Arthur simply made a flying leap to the shore and caught her in his arms.

Then he held her at arm's length, and if eyes could eat, these would have been the last moments upon earth of a very lovely young woman.

Then a sort of horror of what he had done and of what he was doing seized him. His hands dropped to his sides and the pupils of his eyes became pointed with pain. But she said:

"It's all right, Arthur; don't look like that. My husband is dead."

The Seven Darlings

"Dead?" said Arthur, his face once more joyous as an angel's. "Thank God for that!"

And why not thank God when some worthless, cruel man dies? And why not write the truth about him upon his tombstone instead of the conventional lies?

"But why didn't you write to me?" demanded Arthur.

"It had been such a long time since we saw each other. How did I know that you still cared?"

"But how could I stop caring—about you?"

"Couldn't you?"

"Why, I didn't even try," said Arthur. "I just gave it up as a bad job. But how, in the name of all that's good and blessed, do you happen to be in this particular place at this particular time? Did you, by any chance, come by way of the heavens in a 'sweet chariot'? I came to eject trespassers, and I find you!"

"And I came to spy on you, Arthur, and to find out if you still cared. And if you didn't, I was going to tie a stone round my neck and lie down in the lake. Of course, if I'm a trespasser——"

They had moved slowly away from the shore toward the tents. From one of these a languid, humorous voice that made Arthur start hailed them. And through the fly of the tent was thrust a beautiful white hand and the half of a beautiful white arm.

"I can't come out, Arthur," said the voice; "but good-morning to you, and how's the family?"

"Of all people in the world," exclaimed Arthur; "my own beautiful mamma!" And he sprang to the extended hand and clasped it and kissed it.

"Your excellent stepfather," said the voice, "is out walking up an appetite for breakfast. I hope you will be very polite to him. If it hadn't been for him, Cecily would have stayed in London, where we found her. He wormed her secret out of her and brought her to you as a peace-offering."

There was a deep emotion in Arthur's voice as he said:

"Then there shall always be peace between us."

The hand had been withdrawn from the light of day; but the languid, humorous voice continued to make sallies from the brown tent.

"We didn't want to be in the way; so, remembering this bit of property, we just chucked our Somali outfit into a ship, and here we are! I was dreadfully shocked and grieved to hear that you were all quite broke and had started an inn. In New York it is reported to be a great success, is it?"

The Seven Darlings

"Why, I hope so," said Arthur; "I don't really know. Mary's head man. Maud keeps the books; the triplets keep getting into mischief, and Eve, so far as I know, keeps out. As for me, I had an occupation, but it's gone now."

"What was your job, Arthur?"

"My job was to have my arm in imagination where it now is in reality."

"Cecily!" exclaimed the voice. "Is that boy hugging you publicly? Am I absolutely without influence upon manners even among my own tents?"

"Absolutely, Princess!" laughed Cecily.

"Then the quicker I come out of my tent the better! You'll stop to breakfast, Arthur?"

"With pleasure, but shan't I get word to the girls? Of course, they would feel it their duty to call upon you at once."

"I should hope so—as an older woman I should expect that much of them. But, princess or no princess, I refuse to stand on ceremony. In my most exalted and aristocratic moments I can never forget that I am their mother. So after breakfast *I* shall call on *them*."

At this moment, very tall and thin, in gray Scotch tweeds, carrying a very high, foreheady head, there emerged from the forest Prince

The Seven Darlings

Oducalchi, leading by the hand his eight-year-old son, Andrea, and singing in a touching, clear baritone something in Italian to the effect that a certain "Mariana's roses were red and white, in the market-place by the clock-tower!"

Andrea wore a bright-red sweater, carried a fine twenty-bore gun made by a famous London smith, and looked every inch a prince. He had all the Darling beauty in his face and all the Oducalchi pride of place and fame.

"Mr. Darling, I believe?" asked the prince, his left eyebrow slightly acockbill. "I have not had the pleasure of seeing you for some years, but I perceive that you are by way of accepting my peace-offering."

"I was never just to you," said Arthur, a little pale and looking very proud and handsome, "and you have been very good to my mamma and you have been very good to me. Will you forgive me?"

"I cannot do that. There has been nothing to forgive. But I will shake hands with you with all the pleasure in the world—my dear Cecily, does he come up to the memories of him? Poor children, you have had a sad time of it in this merry world! I may call you 'Arthur'? Arthur, this is your half-brother, Andrea. I hope that

The Seven Darlings

you will take a little time to show him the beautiful ways of your North Woods."

Arthur shook hands solemnly with the small boy, and their stanchly met eyes told of an immediate mutual confidence and liking.

"I've always wanted a brother in the worst way," said Arthur.

"So have I," piped Andrea.

And then Princess Oducalchi came out of her tent, and proved that, although her daughters resembled her in features, simplicity, and grace and dignity of carriage, they would never really vie with her in beauty until they had loved much, suffered much, borne children into the world, and remembered all that was good in things and forgotten all that was evil.

"Mamma," said Arthur, "is worth travelling ten thousand miles to see any day, isn't she?"

"On foot," said Prince Oducalchi, "through forests and morasses infested with robbers and wild beasts."

The princess blushed and became very shy and a little confused for a few moments. Then, with a happy laugh, she thrust one hand through her husband's arm, the other through Arthur's, and urged them in the direction of the tent, where breakfast was to be served.

The Seven Darlings

Andrea followed, with Cecily holding him tightly by the hand.

"If we had not been buried in Somaliland at the time," said Arthur's mother, "we would never have let this 'Inn' happen. I'm sure you were against it, Arthur?"

"Of course," said he simply. "But with sister Mary's mind made up, and the rest backing her, what could a poor broken-hearted young man do? And it has worked out better than I ever hoped. I don't mean in financial ways. I mean, the sides of it that I thought would be humiliating and objectionable haven't been. Indeed, it's all been rather a lark, and Mary insists upon telling me that we are a lot better off than we were. We charge people the most outrageous prices! It's enough to make a dead man blush in the dark. And the only complaint we ever had about it was that the prices weren't high enough. So Mary raised them."

"But," objected Prince Oducalchi, "you, and especially your sisters, cannot go on being innkeepers forever. You, I understand, for instance"—and his fine eyes twinkled with mirth and kindness—"are thinking of getting married."

"I am," said Arthur, with so much conviction that even his Cecily laughed at him.

The Seven Darlings

"When I divorced your poor father," said the princess, "he happened to be enjoying one of his terrifically rich moments. So, in lieu of alimony, he turned over a really huge sum of money to me. When I married Oducalchi and told him about the money, he made me put it in trust for you children, to be turned over to you after your father's death. So you see there was never any real need to start the Inn—but of course we were in Africa and so forth and so on— If you've finished your coffee, I'm dying to see the girls. And I'm dying to tell them about the money, and to send all the horrid guests packing!"

"Some of the horrid guests," said Arthur, "won't pack. Of course, the girls think that I only study frogs and plants; but it's a libel. When two and two are thrust into my hands, I put them together, just as really sensible people do. You will find, mamma, a sad state of affairs at the camp."

Princess Oducalchi began to bristle with interest and alarm.

"Andrea," said his father, "have a canoe put overboard for me."

Andrea rose at once and left the breakfast tent.

"Now, Arthur," cried the princess, "tell me everything at once!"

The Seven Darlings

"Gay," said Arthur, "is in love with a young Englishman, and knows that she is. He had to go home to be made an earl; but I think she is expecting him back in a few days, because she is beginning to take an interest in the things she really likes. Mary is in love with Sam Langham, and he with her. They, however, don't know this. Phyllis has forsaken her garden and become a dead-game sport. This she has done for the sake of a red-headed Bostonian named Herring. Lee and a young fellow named Renier are neglecting other people for each other. And our sedate Maud, formerly very much in the company of two fiery Southerners, is now very much in the company of one of them, Colonel Meredith, of South Carolina. The other Carolinian, Mr. Bob Jonstone, sprained his wrist the other day, and it seems that sister Eve was intended by an all-wise Providence to be a trained nurse. But in the case of those last mentioned there are certain mysteries to be solved."

At this moment Andrea appeared at the tent opening and announced in his piping child voice: "The canoe is overboard, papa."

XXX

ANDREA stuck to his big brother like a leech, and insisted upon crossing to The Camp in the same canoe with him and Cecily. To Andrea the possibility of newly engaged persons wishing to be by themselves was negligible. Princess Oducalchi, an old hand on inland waters, took charge of the other canoe, and, like Arthur, in spite of a look of resigned horror on her husband's face, paddled standing up.

Arthur, too happy to make speed, was rapidly distanced by his mother, whose long, graceful figure and charming little, round head he regarded from time to time with great admiration.

"She might be one of my sisters!" he exclaimed to Cecily.

"If she only was," said Cecily, "and the others were only exactly like her, then I shouldn't be a bit frightened."

"Frightened?"

"Wouldn't you be frightened if I had six great angry brothers and you were just going to meet them for the first time?"

277

The Seven Darlings

Arthur smiled steadily and shook his head.

"I'm too happy to be afraid of anything."

"I'm not. The happier I feel the more frightened I feel. And I can feel your sisters picking me all to pieces, and saying what a horrid little thing I am!"

"Little? Haven't I told you that you are exactly the right size?"

"No, you haven't."

"Then I tell you now. I leave it to Andrea. Isn't she exactly the right size, Andrea?"

"Then mamma is too tall."

"No, mamma is exactly the right size for a mamma. In fact, Andrea," exulted Arthur, "on this particular morning of this particular year of grace everything in the world is exactly the right size, except me. I'm not half big enough to contain my feelings. So here goes!"

And the sedate Arthur put back his head, which resembled that of the young Galahad, and opened his mouth, and let forth the most blood-curdling war-whoop that has been sounded during the Christian era.

Cecily clapped her hands to her ears, and Andrea gazed upon his big brother with redoubled admiration.

"Is that like Indians do?" he asked.

The Seven Darlings

"Not at all," said Arthur; "that's what studious and domesticated young men do when they've overslept, and wake up to find the sky blue and the forest green." And once more he whooped terrifically. And Wow, the dog, heard him, and thought he had gone mad; and Uncas, the chipmunk, ran to the top of a tall tree at full speed, down it even faster, and into a deep and safe hole among the roots.

Gay alone was at the float to receive the Oducalchis; but now word of their coming had gone about The Camp, and the remaining Darlings could be seen hurrying up from various directions.

From embracing her mother, Gay turned with characteristic swiftness and sweetness to Cecily, who had just stepped from Arthur's canoe to the float, flung her arms around her, and kissed her.

"I'm not quite sure of your name," she said; "but I love you very much, and you're prettier than all outdoors."

Then Maud came, followed by Eve and Mary, with Lee next and Phyllis last, and they all talked at once, and made much of their mother and Cecily and little Andrea. And they all teased Arthur at once, and showered Oducalchi with polite and hospitable speeches. And he was

279

greatly moved, because he knew very well that these beautiful maidens had loved their own brilliant scapegrace father to distraction, and that it was hard for them to look with kindness upon his successor.

Never, I think, did a mere float, an affair of planks supported by the displacing power of empty casks, have gathered upon it at one time so much beauty, so many delighted and delightful faces.

And now came guides, servants, and camp helpers, to whom Princess Oducalchi had been a kind and understanding mistress in the old days, and then, shyly and hanging back, hoping they were wanted and not sure, Sam Langham, Renier, Herring, the Carolinians, and others, until the float began to sink and there was a laughter panic and a general rush up the gangway to the shore. Here Wow, the dog, did a great deal of swift wagging and loud barking, and Uncas, the chipmunk, from the top of a tree said: "I'm not really angry, but I'm scolding because I'm afraid to come down, and nobody loves me or makes much of me—ever!"

To Arthur, standing a little aside, beaming with pride and happiness, and recording in his heart every pleasant thing which his sisters said to Cecily and every pleasant look they gave her, came Gay presently, and slipped an arm through his.

"I'm so glad," she said.

But there was something in her voice that was not glad, and with one swift glance he read her wistful heart. He pressed her arm, and said:

"I know one poor little kid that's left out in the cold for the moment; one little lion that feels as if it wasn't going to get any martyr; one little sister that a big brother loves and understands a little bit better than any of the others— So there! At the moment every *chacune* has her *chacun*, except one. Moments are fleeting, my dear, and other moments are ahead. I, too, have lived bad, empty, unhappy moments."

"But you always knew that she cared."

"And don't you know about him?"

"I only know that I've seen so many people appear to be idiotically happy at the same time, and it makes me want to cry."

"And for that very reason," said Arthur, "the moments that are ahead will be the happier."

"I wonder," said Gay, and, "I know," said Arthur.

XXXI

THE fact of Arthur's sudden blossoming into a full-fledged and emphatic figure of romance had an unsettling effect upon many of the peacefully disposed minds in The Camp. It is always so when friends, especially in youth, come to partings of ways. Clement, who takes the Low road, cannot but be disturbed at the thought of those possible adventures which lie in wait for Covington, who has fared forth by the High. There was the feeling among many of the young people in the camp that, if they didn't hurry, they might be left behind. Nobody expressed this feeling or acknowledged it or recognized in it anything more than a feeling of unrest; but it existed, nevertheless, and had its effect upon actions and affections.

Renier had been leading a life of almost perfect happiness. For the things that made him happy were the same sort of things that make boys happy. No school; no parental obstructions or admonitions; green-and-blue days filled from

The Seven Darlings

end to end with fishing, sailing, making fires, shooting at marks, and perfecting himself in physical attainments. Add to these things the digestion and the faculties of a healthy boy interested neither in drink, tobacco, nor in any book which failed to contain exciting and chivalrous adventures, and, above all, a companion whose tastes and sympathies were such that she might just as well have been a boy as not.

They were chums rather than sweethearts. It needed a sense of old times coming to an end and new times beginning to make them realize the full depth and significance of their attachment for each other.

There were four of us once "in a kingdom by the sea," and I shall not forget the awful sense of partings and finality, and calamity, for that matter, furnished by a sudden sight of the first flaming maple of autumn.

"I think your mother's a perfect brick," said Renier. "She makes you feel as if she'd known you all your life, and was kind of grateful to you for living."

"I'm rather crazy about the prince," said Lee. "Of course, I oughtn't to be. But I can't help it, and after all he's been awfully good to mamma. Do you believe in divorce?"

The Seven Darlings

"I never did until I saw your mother. She wouldn't ask for anything that she didn't really deserve."

"But it's funny, isn't it," said Lee, "that so many people get on famously together until they are actually married, and then they begin to fight like cats? I knew a girl who was engaged to a man for five years. You'd think they'd get to know each other pretty well in that time, wouldn't you? But they didn't. They hadn't been married six months before they hated each other."

"And that proves," said Renier, "that long engagements are a mistake."

"Smarty!" exclaimed Lee.

"I suppose your brother'll be getting married right away, won't he? Haven't they liked each other for ever so long?"

"M'm!" Lee nodded. "But Arthur never does anything right away. He does too much mooning and wool-gathering. If a united family can get him to the altar in less than a year they'll have accomplished wonders. There's one thing, though—when we do get him married good and proper, he'll stay married. He's like that at all games. It comes natural to him to keep his eyes in the boat. He's got the finest and sweetest nature of any man in this world, *I* think."

The Seven Darlings

"Of course, you except present company?"

"Heavens, yes!" cried Lee, and they both laughed.

Then, suddenly, Lee looked him in the eyes quite solemnly.

"I wasn't fooling," she said, "not entirely. I *do* think you're fine and sweet. I didn't always, but I do now."

There was levity in Renier's words but not in his voice.

"This," he said, "so far has been a perfectly good Tuesday."

"Whatever we do together," said Lee, "you always give me the best of it. It's been a good summer."

"Do you feel as if summer was over, too?"

She nodded.

"That's funny, isn't it? Because it's nowhere near over, is it? Maybe it's the excitement of the Oducalchis' arrival and your brother's engagement. It makes you sort of feel as if there wasn't time to settle back into the regular life and get things going again before the leaves fall."

He spoke. And from the fine striped maple under which they sat there fell, and fluttered slowly into Lee's lap, a great yellowing leaf ribbed with incipient scarlet.

The Seven Darlings

"That only means," said Renier—but there was a kind of awe in his voice—"that this particular tree has indigestion."

And they sat for a time in silence and looked at the leaf. And lo! Arthur came upon them, smiling.

"I was looking for you two," he said. "I thought maybe you'd do me a great favor. I've got to play host, and——"

"Nobody would miss us!" exclaimed Lee.

"They wouldn't?" said Arthur. "I'll bet you anything you like that, during your absence, you will both be mentioned among the missing, by name, at least five times."

"What'll you bet?" asked Lee eagerly. "Nobody ever thinks of *us*. Nobody ever mentions *us*. Nobody even loves *us*. What'll you bet?"

"Anything you like," said Arthur, "and if necessary I will take charge of the five personal mentionings and make them myself!"

Lee shook her head sadly, and said: "Once an accepted lover, always a sure thing, man. Oh, Arthur, how low you have fallen! You used to engineer bets with me for the sheer joy of seeing me win them. But now you are on the make, and it looks as if there was no justice under heaven— Where do you want us to go and what

The Seven Darlings

do you want us to do when we get there? Of course, we'll go; we always do. Everybody sends us on errands, and we always go. The longer the errands the oftener we go. But nobody seems to realize that we might enjoy spending one single solitary afternoon sitting under a striped maple and watching the green leaves turn yellow. Nobody even loves us! But when we are dead there will be the most frightful remorse and sorrow."

Arthur leaned heavily against the stem of the striped maple.

"Your sad case," he said, "certainly cries aloud for justice and redress——"

" 'Kid us along, Bo,' " said Lee; "we love it!"

"I want two people," said Arthur, "for whom I have affection and in whom I have confidence, to go at once to Carrytown in the *Streak* and consult a lawyer upon a matter of paramount importance and delicacy—" He hesitated, and Lee said:

"I pray you, without further ado, continue your piquant narrative."

Then Arthur, in a tone of solemn, confidential eagerness:

"Look here, you two, go to Carrytown, will you, and find out how quickly two people can get married in the State of New York, and what they have to do about licenses and things? Will you? I'll be eternally obliged."

"Of course, we will," exclaimed Lee in sudden excitement. "Are you game?"

"You bet your sweet life I'm game!" cried the vulgar Renier. And a few minutes later the two inseparable school-boyesque chums, whom nobody mentioned, whom everybody sent on errands, and whom nobody even loved, were streaking across the lake in the *Streak*.

There was but the one lawyer in Carrytown and the one stenographer. Their shingles hang one above the other on the face of the one brick building.

At the door of this building Lee suddenly drew back.

"Look here!" she said. "Won't it look rather funny if we march in hand in hand and say: 'Beg pardon, sir, but how do you get married in the State of New York?'"

"It *would* look funny," said Renier, "and I shouldn't wonder if it made us feel funny. But the joke would really be on the lawyer. We could say '*Honi soit qui mal y pense*' to him. Of course, if it would really embarrass you——"

"It wouldn't," said Lee, "*really*."

The Seven Darlings

So they went up a narrow flight of stairs and knocked on the door of room Number Five. There was no answer. So they pushed open the door and entered a square room bound in sheepskin with red-and-black labels. There was nobody in the room, and Lee exclaimed:

"Nobody even loves us."

"He'll be in the back room," said Renier. "I know. Once I swiped a muskmelon from a lawyer's melon-patch, and had to see him about it. *He* was in the back room——"

" 'Counting out his money' ? "

"No; he was drinking whiskey with a judge and a livery-stable keeper, and they were all spitting on a red-hot stove."

"What did he do about the melon ?"

"He told me to can the melon and have a drink. I had already canned the melon as well as I could (I wasn't educated along scientific lines) and my grandmother had promised me any watch I wanted if I didn't drink till I was twenty-one."

"Did you ?"

"I did not."

"Did you get the watch ?"

"I did not."

"Why not ?"

The Seven Darlings

"Grandma reneged. She said she didn't remember making any such promise."

They pushed open a swinging door and entered the back room.

Here, in a revolving chair, sat a stout young man with a red face. Upon his knees sat a stout young woman with a red face. And with something of the consistency with which a stamp adheres to an envelope so the one red face appeared glued to the other red face.

The red face of the stout young man had one free eye which detected the presence of intruders. And the stout young man said:

"Caught with the goods! Jump up, Minnie, and behave yourself!"

Minnie's upspring was almost a record-breaker.

Renier began to stammer:

"I b-b-beg your pardon," he said, "but I thought you might b-b-be able to tell me how to g-g-get married in New York State."

The stout young man rose from his revolving chair; he was embarrassed almost to the point of paralysis, but his mind and mouth continued to work.

"You've come to just the right man," he said, "at just the right time, for information of that sort. First, you hire a stenographer; then you

They pushed open a swinging door and entered the back room

get a mash on her. Then she sits in your lap—
she *will* do it—and then you kiss her. And then
you get a license, and then you curse laws and red
tape for a while, and then you wed. Now, what
you want is a license?"

"Exactly," said Renier. "It—it's for another
fellow."

"Friend of yours?" queried the stout young
man.

"Yes."

"And you want a license for him, not for
yourself?"

Renier nodded.

"At this moment," said the stout young man,
"there are assembled on the long wharf, chewin'
tobacco and cursin', some twenty-five or thirty
marines. Would you mind just stepping down
and telling that to them?"

"I am quite serious," said Renier. "It is my
friend who wants to get married."

"And *you* don't?"

Renier stammered ineffectually.

"Then," said the stout young man, with a
glance at Lee (of the highest admiration), "you're
a gol-darn fool."

And forthwith he was so vulgar as to burst
into a sudden snatch of song:

The Seven Darlings

"Old man Rule was a gol-darn fool,
For he couldn't see the water in the gol-darn pool!"

At the finish of this improvisation the dreadfully confused Minnie went, "Tee-hee!"

And, horror of horrors, that charming boylike companion, Lee Darling, behind whom were well-bred generations, also went suddenly, "Tee-hee."

"Licenses," said the stout young man, "are applied for in room Five. After you, sir; after you, miss."

And, with a waggish expression, he turned to Minnie.

"Be back in five minutes," he said; "try not to forget me, my flighty one."

When they were in the front room, he said:

"Before a license is issued, the licensor must be satisfied as to the preliminaries. Now, then, what can you tell me as to lap sitting and kissings?"

"You," cried Lee, in a sudden blaze of indignation, "are the freshest, most objectionable American I ever set eyes on."

The stout young man turned appealingly to Renier.

"You wouldn't say that," he said; "you'd say I was just typical, wouldn't you, now? And

The Seven Darlings

I wish you would tell her that, though in these backwoods I have been obliged to eschew my Chesterfield, I've got a great big heart in me and mean well."

During the last words of this speech he became appealingly wistful.

"Why," said he to Lee, "just because Minnie and me is stout, don't you think we know heaven when we see it—the empyrean! Yesterday she threw me down, and I says to her: 'Since all my life seems meant for "fails"—since this was written and needs must be—my whole soul rises up to bless your name in pride and thankfulness. Who knows but the world may end tonight?' To-day she sits in my lap and we see which can hug the hardest. Ever try that?"

And suddenly the creature's voice melted and shook. He was a genuine orator, as we Americans understand it, having that within his powers of voice that defies logic and melts the heart.

"Wouldn't you," he said, "even *like* to sit in his lap? Wouldn't you *love* to sit in his lap and be hugged?"

Lee looked to Renier for help, as he to her. And they took a step apiece directly toward each other, and another step. It was as if they had been hypnotized. Suddenly Renier caught Lee's hand in his, and after a moment of looking into his eyes she turned to the stout man, and sang in miraculous imitation of him:

"Young Miss Mule is a gol-darn fool,
But you made her see the water in the gol-darn pool."

"I'll just get a license blank," said the stout young man. "They're in the back room."

"Thank you," said Renier—"if you will, Mr.——"

"Heartbeat!" flashed the stout young man, and left them. And he wasn't lying or making fun that time. For that was his really truly name. And in northern New York people are beginning to think that he is by way of being up to it.

Suddenly Lee quoted from a joke that she and Renier had in common. She said, as if surprised:

" 'Why, there's a table over there!' "

And Renier, his voice suddenly breaking and melting, answered:

" 'Why, so there is—and here's a chair!' "

And Mr. Heartbeat, making a supreme effort to live up to his name, did not return with the license blank for nearly eight minutes. During

The Seven Darlings

those minutes, Renier resolved that in every room in his home there should be at least one revolving chair. And they came out of Mr. Heartbeat's office no longer boyish companions but lovers, a little startled, engaged, and licensed to be married.

XXXII

"LEE, dear," said Renier, "you don't feel that that fellow buncoed you into this, do you? Please say you don't."

"Of course, I wasn't buncoed," she said, and with infinite confidence. "Why, I've seen the thing coming for months! Haven't you?"

"I've seen a certain girl begin by being very dear and grow dearer and dearer—I wish we could *walk* back. I'm afraid of motor-boats, fresh water, and sudden storms on mountain lakes. And I hereby highly resolve that after this perilous trip I shall never again do anything dangerous, such as watching people going up in aeroplanes, such as sitting around with wet feet, such as eating green fruit, such as— Oh, my own darling little kiddie," he whispered with sudden trembling emotion, "but this life is precious."

"George and Charley are looking at us," said Lee, "with funny looks. I wonder if they are *on?* I wonder if everybody will be *on*—just by looking at us. *Do* I look foolish?"

The Seven Darlings

"You do not, but I think you are foolish to take a feller like me, and that's why I'm going to dance down this gang-plank and snap my fingers and shock George and Charley out of their senses."

During this first part of the *Streak's* swift rush from Carrytown to The Camp a tranquil silence came over them. Lee, I think, was searching her heart with questions. But she had no doubt of her love for Renier; she doubted only her capacity to be to him exactly the wife he needed. And I know that Renier just sat, brazening the critical glances of George and Charley, and adored her with his eyes.

And what were his thoughts? Would you give a penny for them? He leaned closer to her, and in a whisper that thrilled them both to the bone, he quoted from Poe:

"And neither the angels in heaven above,
    Nor the demons down under the sea,
Can ever dissever my soul from the soul
    Of the beautiful Annabel Lee."

And a little later he said:

"I never knew till to-day what poetry is for. I thought people who wrote it were just a little simple and that people who read and quoted it were perfect jackasses."

The Seven Darlings

"And what is poetry for?" asked Lee, smiling.

"Poetry," he said, "is for *you*."

As they neared the camp the sentiment in their hearts yielded a little to excitement.

"When we tell 'em," said Lee, "it's going to be just like a bomb going off. And everybody will be terribly envious."

"Nobody even loves us," laughed Renier, and he quoted:

> "Among ten million, one was she,
> And surely all men hated me."

And like a flash Lee answered:

> "Among ten million he was one,
> So all the ladies fought like fun."

"One thing is sure," said Renier, "we've more than executed Brother Arthur's delicate and confidential commission. What we don't know about getting married in the State of New York simply doesn't exist."

Arthur, eager and impatient, was like a more famous person, watching and waiting.

"Well," he said, "thank you a thousand times. And what did you find out?"

"We've brought you a license blank," said Lee; "you simply fill it out with your names and ages and things—like this—" And she placed a second paper in her brother's hands.

And conspicuous on the paper he saw Lee's name and Renier's. His hands shook a little, and his face became very grave and tender.

"Say you're surprised!" exclaimed Lee; "say you were never so surprised in all your born days!"

"But I'm not surprised," said Arthur. "Come here to me!" He opened his arms to her and she flung herself into them. Over her shoulder and hiding head Arthur spoke to Renier.

"No man," he said, "knows his own heart, and no woman knows hers. Nobody can promise with honesty to love forever. For sometimes love dies just as simply and inexplicably as it is born. But a man can promise to be good to his wife always, and tender with her and faithful to her, and if he is a gentleman he will make those promises good."

"I make those promises," said Renier simply; "will you give her to me?"

"It is for no man to give or to withhold," said Arthur. "The gods give. The duty of brothers is just to try to help things along and to love their sisters and to be friends with their brothers-in-law."

XXXIII

" AND now," said Lee, "I think I'll tell
mamma."

On the way to find the princess, Lee and Renier
encountered Herring. He appeared to be hurrying, but something in their faces brought him to
a sudden stop.

Their attempts to meet his inquiring gaze
with indifference proved unavailing, for he closed
one eye and said:

"Which of you two has swallowed the family
canary? Or has each of you swallowed half of
him?"

The guilty pair were unable to preserve their
natural coloring. They turned crimson, and each
showed a courteous willingness to let the other be
the first to speak.

"You've been to Carrytown," said Herring.
"I saw you start. You raced down to the float.
And in your rivalry to see which should board
the *Streak* first, it looked as if you were going to
knock each other overboard. Renier, he won,
and you, Miss Lee, were annoyed. When you

returned from Carrytown, you had long, pensive, anxious faces. Renier stepped ashore and, in helping you ashore, gave you both hands. When a girl whom I have seen climb a tree after a baby owl accepts the aid of a man's two hands in stepping from a solid boat to a solid float, there is food for thought. Having landed, you proceeded direct to the head of the Darling family and were for some time engaged with him in solemn discourse. A paper was shown him. From a distance it looked as if it might be some sort of a license—a license to hunt and be hunted, perhaps——"

"But it wasn't," said Lee suddenly, and she thrust her hand under Renier's arm. "If you must know, Mr. Sherlock Holmes, it was a license to love and be loved. So there!"

She was no longer blinking, nor was Renier. They looked so loving and proud that it was Herring's turn to feel embarrassment. Then he said:

"I only meant to be a tease. If I'd really thought anything—I wouldn't, of course; none of my darn business. But I'm *awfully* glad. I've hoped all along it would happen. It's the best ever. Am I to be secret as the grave or can I tell—any one I happen to meet?"

The Seven Darlings

"Give us ten minutes to tell mamma," said Lee, "and then consider your lips unsealed."

Herring had drawn from his pocket a stop-watch and set it going.

"Ten minutes," he said. "Thanks awfully! And good luck!"

He had turned, waving his free hand to them, and darted away.

Lee laughed scornfully.

"Any one he happens to meet!" she exclaimed. "He's headed straight for the garden, and there he'll just *happen* to meet Phyllis. She was speaking of her tomatoes at breakfast, and saying that they ought to be ripening and that she was going to have a look at them."

"Lee, darling," said Renier, "nobody can possibly see us. And when Mr. Heartbeat left us alone in the front room it was a frightfully long time ago. And sometimes a fellow's arms get to aching with sheer emptiness, and—and, 'this is the forest primeval, the murmuring pines and the hemlocks——' "

"Are mostly birches and larches hereabouts," said Lee, and, with a happy laugh, she drifted into a pair of arms that closed tightly about her. And, "It doesn't matter if anybody does see us," she said.

•   •   •   •   •   •   •   •

The Seven Darlings

It was characteristic of Herring that he should enter the garden by leaping over the fence. It was also characteristic that he should catch his foot on the top rail and fall at full length in a bed of very beautiful and much cherished phlox.

Phyllis, in the path near by, gazed at the fallen man with mirth and anxiety.

"Hurt?" she asked.

He rose and examined a watch which he was carrying in his right hand.

"Crystal smashed," he said, "but still going. And I've got to wait four minutes!"

"Why have you got to wait four minutes?"

"Because I promised to wait ten, and six of them have elapsed. Oh, but won't you be excited when I am at liberty to speak! It's more exciting than when we were lost in the woods, crossing the swamp that had never been crossed before. Meanwhile, let us calm ourselves by talking of something prosaic. How are the tomatoes getting on?"

Phyllis put up her hand in a smiling military salute.

" 'General Blank's compliments,' " she said, " 'and the colored troops are turning black in the face.' "

"My favorite breakfast dish," said Herring,

"is grilled tomatoes, preceded by raw oysters and oatmeal."

"Isn't it nice," said Phyllis, "that there is money in the family after all, and we're going to give up The Camp as an inn?"

"It would have been given up anyway," said Herring. "A determined body of men had so resolved in secret. There's one minute left."

For some reason they found nothing to say during the whole of that minute. When the last second thereof had passed forever, Herring said simply:

"Your sister Lee and Renier are going to be married."

I cannot describe the expression that came over Phyllis's face. It wasn't exactly jealousy; it wasn't exactly the expression of a beautiful female commuter who has just missed her train. It wasn't a wild look, or a happy look, or a sad look. Perhaps it was a little bit more of an aching void look than anything else.

Whatever its exact nature, the wily Herring studied it with an immense satisfaction. And then his heart began to flurry in a sort of panic.

"Lee!" exclaimed Phyllis, "married! Why, they're nothing but children!"

She felt something encircle her waist. She

"Lee!" exclaimed Phyllis, "married! Why, they're nothing but children!"

The Seven Darlings

looked down and saw a hand and part of an arm.

"What are you doing?" she asked, in a sort of daze.

"I'm trying to establish a hold on you," said Herring, and toward the end of so saying his voice broke; "and you're not to feel lonely and deserted with me standing here, are you?"

For a moment it seemed to Herring that Phyllis was going to extricate herself from his encircling arm. She achieved, indeed, a quarter revolution to the left and away from him.

"Don't, Phyllis!" he cried. "Don't do it! I couldn't bear it!"

Then she ceased revolving to the left, stopped, and from a startled, uncertain, half-frightened young person became suddenly a warmly loving young person, warmly loved, who revolved suddenly to the right, and became the recipient of a sudden storm of ecstatic exclamations and kisses.

And then, nestling close to the one and only man in the world, she listened with complete satisfaction to his efforts to explain to her just how beautiful and wonderful and good she was.

XXXIV

WHEN Lee and Renier, locked in each other's arms, stood in the forest primeval, they were mistaken in imagining themselves to be unobserved.

A short half-hour before, Mary Darling had received a proposal of marriage. But Mr. Sam Langham, usually so worldly-wise, had erred, perhaps, in his choice of time and place. Whatever a huge kitchen, bright with sunlight upon burnished copper, may be, it is not a romantic place. And, worse than this, Mary herself was not in a romantic mood. Certain supplies due by the morning express had not arrived. Chef was at the telephone shouting broken French to the butcher in Carrytown; one of the kitchen-maids had come down with an aching tooth, and the other had been sent upon an errand from which she should have long since returned.

"Oh," exclaimed Mary, as Mr. Langham entered, smiling, "everything is in such a mess! I don't believe there's going to be any lunch to-day for any one. And I think I shall have a nervous breakdown!"

The Seven Darlings

"I told you you would long ago," said Langham, "if you didn't rest more and take things easier. What *does* it matter if things go wrong once in a while? And if there isn't going to be any lunch, I'm glad, for one. I was thinking of not eating mine, anyway. And if *I'm* not hungry, you can be pretty sure that nobody else is hungry. I tell you it hurts me to see you work so hard. I admire it and I bow down, but it hurts. You tell Chef to do the best he can, and you come for a brisk walk with me. We'll walk up an appetite, and——"

"I can't *possibly*," said Mary. "I've got to stand by."

"Then you go for a walk and I'll stand by. Only trust me. *I'll* see that nobody goes hungry."

She did not appear to have heard his offer, and Mr. Langham spoke again, with a sudden change of tone.

"I'd like to take you out of this. I'd like to make everything in the world easy for you, if you would only let me. But you know that. You've known it all along. And knowing it, you've never even shown that it interested you; and so I suppose it's folly for me to mention it. But a man can't give up all his hopes of happiness in this world without even stating them, can he? I've hoped that you might get to care a little about me——"

Mary interrupted him with considerable impatience.

"Really," she said, "with Chef shouting at the telephone, and all, I don't know what you are driving at."

At that Mr. Langham looked so hurt and so unhappy and woebegone that Mary was touched with remorse.

"I didn't realize you were in earnest," she said. "I'm sorry I've hurt your feelings, but it's no use. I'm sorry—awfully sorry; but it's no use."

"I'm sorry, too," said Langham; "sorry I spoke; sorrier there was no use in speaking; sorriest of all that I'm no good to any one. But as long as I had to come a cropper, why, I'm glad it was for no one less wonderful than you. Will you let things be as they were? I won't bother you about my personal feelings ever again by a look or a word."

After he had gone Mary stood for a while with knitted brows. Chef had finished telephoning. The kitchen was in silence. Suddenly she broke this silence.

"Chef," she exclaimed, "I'm no use at all!

The Seven Darlings

You'll just have to do the best you can about lunch by yourself."

And she left the kitchen with great swiftness, looking like an angel on the verge of tears.

Chef's shining red face divided into a white smile, and he began to bustle about and make a noise with pots and pans and carving tools, and to sing as he bustled:

> "*Sur le pont d'Avignon*
> *L'on y danse, l'on y danse,*
> *Sur le pont d'Avignon*
> *L'on y danse tout en rond—*
> *Les belles dames font comm' ça,*
> *Et puis encore comm' ça.*"

It is probable that in his gay Parisian youth Chef had known a good deal about *les belles dames*. He had latterly given much attention to the progress of Miss Darling's friendship with Mr. Langham, and that this same progress had received a sharp setback under his very nose concerned him not a little. Chef possessed altogether too much currency that had once belonged to that lavish tipper, Mr. Langham. And Chef did not wish Mr. Langham to be driven from the kitchen and The Camp. He wished Mr. Langham to become a permanent Darling asset—like himself and the French range. And so, half singing, half speaking, and furiously bustling, he announced:

"I'll show her how little difference she makes. Without advice or dictation, practically without supplies of any kind, I shall arrange, *nom de Dieu!* a luncheon which, for pure deliciousness, will not have been surpassed during the entire Christian era. I shall hint to her that I tolerate her in my kitchen because I have known her since she was a little girl, but I shall make it clear by words and deeds that her presence or absence is not of the least importance. Let her then turn for comfort to the worthy, generous, and rich Mr. Langham, for whom the mere poaching of an egg is an exquisite pleasure!"

And he frowned and began to think formidable and inventive thoughts about matters connected with his craft and immediate needs and necessities.

Mary Darling had, of late, often imagined herself receiving an offer of marriage from Mr. Langham. That is badly expressed. Only the most insufferable and self-sufficient of men make offers of marriage. Your true, modest, and chivalrous lover gets down on his real or figurative knees and begs and beseeches. She had, then,

often imagined her hand in the act of being be-
sought by Mr. Langham. Being a practical young
woman, she had pictured this as happening (re-
peatedly) at sunset, by moonlight, in the depths
of romantic forests or on the tops of romantic
mountains. And some voice in her (some very
practical voice) told her that it never should have
happened in a kitchen.

Mr. Langham's "sweet beseeching," instead of
"moving her strangely," had made her rather
cross. And such tenderness as she usually had
for him had fled to cover. But now, as the clean,
green forest closed about her, she had a reaction.
She came to a dead stop and realized that she had
been through an emotional crisis. Her heart was
beating as if she had just finished a steep, swift
climb. And her heart was aching too, aching for
the kind and gentle friend and well-wisher to
whom she had been so inexplicably cold and
cutting. It was in vain to mourn for that dia-
mond of a heart which she had rejected with so
much finality. He had said that he would never
"bother" her again (*Bother* her! The idea!), and
he never would. He was a man of his word, Sam
Langham was. Perhaps, even now he was causing
his things to be packed with a view to leaving The
Camp for ever and a day. But what could she

The Seven Darlings

do? Could she go to him (in person or by writing)
and in his presence eat as much as a single mouth-
ful of humble-pie? No, she could not possibly
do that. Then, what could she do? Well, with
the usual negligible results, she could cry her eyes
out over the spilt milk.

She went swiftly forward, the shadows dappling
her as she went, and her heart swelling and swelling with self-pity and general miserableness.
Thoughts of Arthur and his happiness flashed
through her mind. The thought that she, Mary
Darling, unmarried, would in the course of a few
years be called an old maid, caused her a panicky
feeling. She pictured herself as very old (and
very ugly), exhibiting improbable Chinese dogs at
dog-shows and scowling at rosy babies. And I
must say she almost laughed.

The path turned sharply to the right and dis-
closed to Mary's eyes two young people who
stood locked in each other's arms and rocked
slightly from side to side—rocked with ineffable
delight and tenderness.

She stood stock-still, in plain view if they had
looked her way, until presently they unlocked arms,
drew a little apart, and had a good long look at
each other, and then turned their backs upon that
part of the forest and departed slowly.

The Seven Darlings

Whither she was going, Mary did not know. But she went very swiftly and had upon her face the expression of a beautiful female commuter who has arrived at the station just in time to see her train pull out. But this expression changed when she found her path blocked by the diminutive house in which Sam Langham lived, and saw Sam Langham, a look of wonder on his face, rise from his big piazza chair and come toward her.

"Lee and Renier are going to be married," she exclaimed, all out of breath, "and I didn't mean to be such a brute! And I wouldn't have hurt you for anything in the world!"

Sam Langham only looked at her, for he was afraid to speak.

"I'm just an old goose," said Mary humbly, but very bravely, "and I take everything back. And if you meant what *you* said, Sam, and want to begin all over again, why, don't just stand there and look at me."

And presently she was ashamed of herself for having been so forward, and so she pursued the feelings of shame to their logical conclusion and hid her face.

And now, for the first time, she realized how hard she had worked ever since The Camp was changed into an inn to make it a go, and how

The Seven Darlings

much she needed rest and comforting and a masculine executive to lean on.

"Who said," murmured the ecstatic Langham, "that nothing good ever came of liking good things to eat?"

"Sam," said Mary, "I'm so happy I don't care if lunch is burned to a cinder."

It wasn't. Out of odds and ends of raw materials, and great slugs and gallons of culinary genius, Chef produced a lunch that transcended even Mary's and Langham's belief in him.

But it was Arthur who insisted that champagne be opened; and perhaps the champagne made the lunch seem even more delicious than it really was.

Maud and Eve had already discounted Arthur's engagement and Lee's. They had not, it is true, learned of the latter without feeling that if they didn't hurry they would miss their train; but they had disguised and fought off that feeling until now they were their gay and natural selves. It remained for Mr. Langham to shock them suddenly into a new set of emotions.

"I should be obliged," said he, rising to his feet, with a glass of champagne in his hand, "if everybody would drink the health of the happiest man present." Arthur and Renier looked very self-

314

The Seven Darlings

conscious. But Mr. Langham concluded: "And that man is myself. I have the honor to announce that, beyond peradventure, the loveliest and sweetest girl in all the world——"

And at that Mary blushed so and looked so happy and beautiful that everybody shouted with joy and surprise and laughter, and drank champagne, and tossed compliments about like shuttle-cocks. And Arthur and Renier and Langham had a violent dispute as to which was the happiest; and decided to settle the dispute with sabres at—twenty paces.

Her first burst of surprise and excitement and pleasure having passed, Eve Darling experienced a sudden sinking feeling. She felt as if all the people she most loved to be with were going away on a delightful excursion and that she was being left behind. It was at this moment, while the uproar was still at its height, that she heard the shaken voice of Mr. Bob Jonstone in her ear.

"How about us?" he demanded.

"How about us—what?" she answered.

Then she felt her hand seized and held in the secret asylum furnished by the table-cloth, and there stole over her the solaceful feeling of having been asked at the last moment to go upon the delightful excursion.

The Seven Darlings

"Eve?"

"Eve, darling—is it all right?"

"All right."

And then up shot Mr. Jonstone like a projectile from a howitzer, and he cried aloud, his habitual calmness and lazy habit of speech flung to the winds.

"You're not the only happy men in the world," he shouted. "I'm happier than the three of you put together, I am! Because my Darling is the best and most beautiful of all Darlings, and if any man dares to gainsay that, let him just step outside with me for five minutes—that's all."

Colonel Meredith's hair bristled like the mane of a fighting terrier.

"Do you mean to say," he whispered to Maud in a sort of savage whisper, "that I've got to swallow that insult without protest?"

It was on the tip of Maud's tongue to say that she didn't know what he meant. But how could she say that when she knew perfectly well?

"Only give me the right to answer him," continued the sincere warrior. He rose to his feet. "Is it yes—or no?"

"It's yes—yes," exclaimed Maud and, horrified with herself, she leaned back blushing and full of wonder.

The Seven Darlings

"Mr. Jonstone—Mr. Bob—Jonstone!" cried Colonel Meredith.

Mr. Jonstone's attention was presently attracted, and he gave his cousin a glittering look.

"I'll be only too delighted to step outside with you for five minutes," said Colonel Meredith.

And the cousins glared and glared at each other. But whether or not they were really in earnest, if only for a moment, will never be known; at any rate, each of them appeared suddenly to perceive something comic about the other, and both burst into peals of schoolboy laughter.

Only Gay's happiness seemed a little forced, and her mother's.

XXXV

GAY hardly slept at all. She was at her window half the night asking troubled questions of the stars and of the moon and of the moonlight on the lake. She had not, during the summer, taken her sisters' affairs very seriously, perhaps because she was so seriously engrossed with her own. She had, even in her heart, almost accused them of flirting and carrying on lest time hang heavy on their hands. Her own romance she had supposed all along to be real, the others mere reflections of romantic places and situations. But it began to look as if only her own romance had been spurious. It was a long time since she had heard from Pritchard. He had told her very simply that he was now the Earl of Merrivale, and that, as soon as certain things were settled and arranged, he intended to return to America. After that, there had been no word from him of any kind. She tried to comfort herself with the thought that if he was that kind of man—blow hot, blow cold—she was well rid of him, and she failed dismally.

The Seven Darlings

A man is in love with a certain girl. He learns that she is vain, gay, extravagant, heartless, and going to marry some other man. Does any of this comfort him? Not if he is in love with her, it doesn't. Not a bit.

So Gay could say to herself: "He's thoughtless and inconstant, and I'm well out of it!" She could say that, and she did say that, and then she buried her face in her pillow and cried very quietly and very hard.

She was up before the sun.

It would have taken more than one night of wakefulness and weeping to leave marks upon that lovely face which sudden cold water and the resolution to suffer no more could not erase.

But she had not rowed a mile or more before the color in her cheeks was really vivid again and the whites of her eyes showed no traces of tears.

She did not know why she was rowing or whither. It was as if some strong hand had forced her from bed before sunrise, forced her into her fishing-clothes, forced her into a guide boat, placed oars in her hands, and compelled her to row.

She even smiled, wondering where she was going.

"I can go anywhere I like," she thought; "but I don't want to go anywhere in particular, and yet

The Seven Darlings

I am quite obviously on my way to somewhere or other. I'm like Alice in Wonderland. I think I'll go to Carrytown and get the morning mail."

But she had no sooner beached toward Carrytown than the distance there seemed unutterably long, especially for a rower who had yet to breakfast.

"I know," thought Gay at last; "I'll row to Placid Brook and see if the big trout is still feeding in his private preserve. I'll land just where we did before and cross the meadow and spy on him from behind a bush. I wish I'd brought some tackle. I'd like to catch him and cook him for my breakfast—so I would!"

Upon this resolution, the work of rowing became very light. It was as if the force which had started her upon the excursion had had Placid Brook in mind all the time.

Having laid her course for the meadow at the mouth of Placid Brook, she kept the stern of the boat in direct line with a distant mountain-top, and so held it. The sun was now peeping over the rim of the world, and here and there morning breezes were darkening and dappling the burnished surface of the lake.

Now and then, as she neared the meadow, Gay glanced over her shoulder, once for quite a long time, resting on her oars, because she thought she saw a doe with a fawn. They turned out to be nothing more tender than a couple of granite rocks. And once again she rested on her oars and looked for a long time—not this time upon the strength of a hallucination, but of an impulse.

She followed this inconsequential act with a long sigh, and enough strokes of the oar to bring her to land.

When she stood upright on the meadow she could see the very spot from which Pritchard had cast for the big trout. And she saw (and had a curious dilating of the heart at the same moment) that that particular spot of meadow was once more occupied by a human being—or were her eyes and her breakfastless stomach playing tricks?

A young man in rusty meadow-colored clothes appeared to be kneeling with his back toward her. She advanced swiftly toward him, curious only of a great wonder and an indescribable (and possibly fatal) beating of her heart. And suddenly she knew that her man was real and no hallucination, for she perceived at her feet the stub of a Turkish cigarette, still smoking. Then she called to him:

"Halloo, there!"

The Earl of Merrivale started as if he had been

shot at, then leaped to his feet and turned to-ward her with a cry of joy.

"What are you doing here?" he cried.

And they had approached to within touching distance of each other.

"I don't know," she said. "What are you?"

"It was too early to pay calls," he said, "so I thought I'd have one more whack at the big char and bring him to you for a present. But tell me —does our bet still stand?"

He looked at her so tenderly and lovingly and hopefully that she hadn't the heart to be anything but tender and loving herself.

"The bet still stands," she said, "if you win. I've missed you terribly."

"I took him," said the earl. "I was just weighing him when you called. He weighs a lot more than three pounds. So I win."

"Yes, you win."

"And the bet still stands?"

She nodded happily.

"And you won't renege—you'll pay? You'll be Countess of Merrivale?"

"If you want me to be," she said humbly.

"If I want you to be!"

And she had imagined herself so often in his arms that she was not now surprised or troubled to find herself there.

The Seven Darlings

"I was so unhappy," she said; "and now I'm so happy."

And after a little while she said:

"I'd like to see him."

Presently they stood looking down at the great trout.

"He's done a lot for us, hasn't he?" said Gay. "He was the beginning of things. And it seems sort of a pity——"

"He's still breathing. He'll live if we put him back. Shall we?"

"Yes, please."

There was plenty of life and fight in the old trout. He no sooner felt that water was somewhere under him than he gave a triumphant, indignant flop, tore himself from Merrivale's hands, and disappeared with a splendid, smacking splash.

"Good old boy!" laughed Merrivale.

"And yet," said Gay, "it's a pity that we couldn't take him back to camp and show him off. He was the biggest trout I ever saw."

"He wasn't a trout, dear," said Merrivale; and he grinned lovingly at her. "He was a char."

"Of course he was," said Gay humbly; "I forgot."

XXXVI

I WISH I could write first, "The Seven Darlings lived happily ever afterward," and then the word "Finis." But I cannot end so easily and maintain a reputation for veracity. They can't have lived happily afterward until they are dead —can they? At the moment they have just closed The Camp after the summer and scattered to their winter homes; that is, all of them except Gay.

The Camp, of course, is no longer an inn. They run it on joint account for themselves and for their friends. And they have delightful times.

Colonel Meredith has built a tremendous house on his ancestral acres, and during the winter Arthur and his wife, the Herrings, the Reniers, the Jonstones, and the Langhams are apt to make it their headquarters.

Gay and her young man were to have visited the Merediths this winter. There was going to be a united family effort to discover the buried silver which Mr. Bob Jonstone sold to his cousin, but of course the great war has upset this excellent plan, together with a good many million other plans, even more excellent and important.

The Earl of Merrivale is fighting somewhere in the wet ditches—Gay doesn't know exactly where. She herself, a red cross on her sleeve, is with one of the field-hospitals, working like a slave to save life. Because her husband is an Englishman, she didn't think that she could ever be kind to a German or an Austrian, but that turned out to be a whopping big error of judgment. They all look alike to her now, and her heart almost breaks over them. But I don't know what will become of her if anything happens to Merrivale. I think poor little Gay would just curl up and die. He is all the world to her, just as she is to him.

Well, they are only one loving couple out of a good many hundred thousands. The times are too momentous to follow them further or waste words and sympathy on them. The world is thinking in big figures, not in units.

Only a sentimentalist here and there regards as more important than empire and riches the little love-affairs that death is hourly ending, and the little babies who are never to be born.

www.ingramcontent.com/pod-product-compliance
Lightning Source LLC
Chambersburg PA
CBHW032229010726
47494CB00002B/422